WANTED: SAM BASS

GREAT WESTERN DETECTIVE LEAGUE

WANTED: SAM BASS

PAUL COLT

FIVE STAR

A part of Gale, Cengage Learning

GALE
CENGAGE Learning·

Farmington Hills, Mich • San Francisco • New York • Waterville, Maine
Meriden, Conn • Mason, Ohio • Chicago

GALE
CENGAGE Learning·

LIBRARY OF CONGRESS CATALOGING-IN-PUBLICATION DATA

Colt, Paul.
    Wanted: Sam Bass / Paul Colt. — First edition.
        pages ; cm. — (Great western detective league ; 1)
    ISBN 978-1-4328-2938-4 (hardcover) — ISBN 1-4328-2938-6
(hardcover)
        1. Law enforcement—United States—History—19th century—
Fiction. I. Title.
PS3603.O4673W36 2015
813'.6—dc23   2014031285

First Edition. First Printing: January 2015
Find us on Facebook– https://www.facebook.com/FiveStarCengage
Visit our website– http://www.gale.cengage.com/fivestar/
Contact Five Star™ Publishing at FiveStar@cengage.com

Printed in the United States of America
1 2 3 4 5 6 7 19 18 17 16 15

WANTED: SAM BASS

PROLOGUE

Deadwood
August 1877

The No. 10 Saloon catered to rough mining types and the assorted gamblers, gunmen, scoundrels and soiled doves ready to help a man with an itch out of his hard-earned poke. Sam Bass confined his interest to playing cards with a couple of Manuel Homestake miners he considered easy marks, much to the disappointment of more than a few of the whores. A handsome devil by the doves' estimation, he wore a frock coat over a slight frame. He had dark wavy hair barbered close with a curled mustache. His cool gray eyes gave the doves a flutter. Others thought more of his cross draw double rig. The guns bore him a fearsome reputation that served to keep his card playing peaceful. If the cards ran against him, he could count on the Colts to stake him to a new game.

Hank Schott, foreman at the Homestake came to the No. 10 for his usual payday sport. Bass drew him into his game for the price of a drink. Schott enjoyed some celebrity owing to his position at the richest mine in the Black Hills. He was free to impress his importance on any that might care to listen. Liquor improved his self-importance. It didn't help his hand at cards. The handsome Texan in the frock coat seemed only too happy to listen, pour and win.

Bass fanned his cards and shoved in his bet. "Two dollars."

Hank squinted at his cards. "Two dollars, make it three." The other two miners checked to Bass.

"I'll see your three and raise you two more."

Schott scratched the stubble on his chin. "Goes again' my better judgment, but I'll see and call."

"Full house, ladies and gents." Bass laid down queens and jacks.

Schott tossed over two pair. "Dad burn it! I'd best scratch my itch while I still got some payday left to scratch it with." He stretched and yawned. "Besides I got a long day comin' tomorrow."

Bass laughed as he raked in his pot. "What makes tomorrow longer than any other day at the mine?"

The miner shook his head. "Puttin' up a shipment. You got to get all the weights and measures and tallies right for the manifest. All that cipherin's enough to make a man's head hurt." He scraped his chair back.

Bass tossed in his cards. *Long day putting up a shipment sounds like a big one.*

"That'll be enough for me, boys." He cast around the smoky saloon until he spotted his partner at a back corner table. Joel Collins sat under a buxom redhead bent on tickling his fancy. A smaller man, Collins aspired to make up for his lack of stature by associating with a hard case like Bass. He had an ornery disposition, hot temper and enough of a gun hand to cause trouble he couldn't always finish. Bass tolerated the little gunny because he mostly did what he was told when he was sober. The half-empty bottle and two glasses on the table told that story for the night. Collins's share of a fraudulent cattle sale amounted to enough for the whore to fall in love with him, at least until the money ran out. Bass crossed the crowded saloon and interrupted the opening act to a trip upstairs.

"Joel."

"Not now, Sam. I'm busy." He plainly enjoyed a handful of

warm willing flesh.

"Maybe not now, but be ready to ride at sunup."

"Sunup?" He cocked an eye over the lace frill at a brimming bodice.

"Sunup. We got work to do."

"What work?"

"Come along now if you want to know, otherwise I'll tell you in the morning."

"I'm already comin' along. I'll see you in the morning."

"Suit yourself. Just don't be late."

Cheyenne & Deadwood Stage Road

Slanting sun crested the pine-blackened hills in the east. Bass and Collins rode south out of town. Collins nursed the whiskey-hazed effects of the night before, trying to remember if she'd been worth it. The fact that he couldn't made the harsh light of day all the worse for it. He let the miles roll by, suffering his private misery in silence.

Bass set a blistering pace from the moment they cleared the outskirts of town. He held to the stage road, deviating only to skirt the rest stops spaced at ten-mile intervals along the run between Cheyenne and Deadwood. Most stops offered few comforts beyond a small station, privy and corrals where the relief teams were stabled. Somewhat larger stations placed at forty-mile intervals offered passengers and stage hands the comfort of a small lounge where simple meals were served.

At midday, Bass mercifully drew a halt beside a roadside stream to rest and water the horses. They stepped down. Collins splashed water in his face clearing enough of his head to overcome some of his misery.

"Where the hell are we going and what's the hurry?"

"Back from the dead, are we? You have a good time last night?"

"Must have. A man don't generally feel so poorly unless he done something to deserve it. Now answer my questions."

"Like I said last night, we got a job."

Collins rubbed the bridge of his nose between a thumb and forefinger in a futile attempt to staunch the throbbing behind his eyes. "What kind of job?"

"We're gonna hit the Deadwood to Cheyenne stage tomorrow."

"Oh. Why?"

"Well, while you was fixin' to get yourself a poke last night, I was busy workin'."

"Workin' hell, you was playin' cards."

"I'm surprised you remember. One of my marks was a talkative foreman at the Homestake."

Collins set aside his misery at the mention of a gold strike that rich.

"There's a big shipment headed south on the stage tomorrow. I mean to take it."

"Uh-huh. So there's the stage road. What's the hurry?"

Bass shook his head, suffering the fool. "I don't mean to just take it. I mean to keep it."

"What's that got to do with bustin' our butts in the saddle? We tryin' to beat the stage to Cheyenne?"

"The nearest law is Cheyenne. We need to find a spot to hit the stage and make a clean getaway. We got until midday tomorrow to find us that spot. Now mount up. We got ground to cover."

Two miles north of the southbound forty-mile stop, they found a spot where the stage road climbed a steep rise that curved through a narrow rock gulch. Bass drew rein to have a look. A southbound stage would come into the curve blind with no room to maneuver. They'd have to slow down for the grade with a team so close to the end of a ten-mile run. Two riders blocking the road could stop the stage. It looked like easy pickings as long as the shotgun messenger didn't go all heroic on them. After that it was a matter of making good their getaway.

They found a sheltered crevice east of the gulch to keep them out of sight of any northbound traffic while they waited. Collins's head cleared by late afternoon, restoring him to his more talkative self.

"Where we headed after we hit this stage?"

Bass fished the makings out of his coat pocket. "Ready for more of what got you last night already?"

"I'm always ready for a good time. Where's it gonna be?"

"South." He rolled his smoke and tucked it between his lips.

"South. South covers a lot of ground."

Bass scratched a match and puffed. He spit a bit of tobacco off his tongue, clearing the way for his answer. "If anybody comes lookin' for us, it'll likely come out of Cheyenne. If we head southeast it's about the same as doublin' back on 'em. We'll be long gone before anybody figures that out."

"Smart."

"Somebody's got to be. We'd starve sure as hell if we was to rely on you playin' cards."

Collins scowled in reply. "I reckon I'll rustle up some firewood for supper."

"No fire. We ain't puttin' up smoke sign that tells anyone with a curiosity we're here."

"What about supper?"

"Hardtack and jerky, now shut up and get some sleep."

Morning sun climbing the eastern sky told Bass it was time to take up the watch.

"Climb up them rocks over yonder and keep your eyes peeled for that stage. You can wake me when you got sign of it."

"Me? Why me? You got eyes too."

"You earn your share your way and I earn mine my way."

"My way seems to include all the work. What's your way?"

"I think for both of us. Now get your ass up them rocks and sing out when you see somethin'."

"Hey-up haw!" Pete Daley slapped lines. The horses labored as they neared the end of their leg on this run. Daley was tired too. Four more legs before he'd get his relief. A drink, a meal and a good night's sleep would all sit pretty good after a long day's drive. He'd have a day's rest before picking up the northbound for the run back to Deadwood.

Joe Harris, the Wells Fargo shotgun messenger, sat beside him in the box. Now and then his head jerked as he fought the rock and pitch of the stage in a failed effort to stay awake. *Some guard*, Pete thought. It'd serve him right if he fell off the damn box. That'd wake him up, or break his neck.

Up ahead the road climbed to a narrow passage winding between the rock walls of a gulch bending west. The team slowed, pulling into the climb. Pete drew lines, bending the team to the turn. The coach swayed as they rounded the curve. A pair of masked bandits with guns drawn blocked the road. The tired team checked its pace at the sight of them. Pete hauled lines. He had no place to run even if the horses had anything left which they didn't. Harris snapped awake too late to make a play for his shotgun. Daley set the brake. One of them yanked the coach door open.

"Nobody in here."

The tall one in the lead leveled a .44 at Daley. "Throw down the strongbox and nobody gets hurt."

"Do like he says, Joe," Daley said, holding the team.

The Wells Fargo man scowled.

"Throw down the damn box, Joe. It ain't worth dyin' for."

Harris climbed up on the roof of the coach and walked back to the boot. He hefted the locked strongbox out and tossed it into the road. The bandit beside the passenger door wheeled his horse to the back of the coach and stepped down. Harris started back to the box. He jumped when the unexpected shot exploded in the narrow confines of the gulch. The padlock shattered with a metallic plink. The bullet whined away.

"Looks like we struck pay dirt," the shooter announced checking the contents of the box.

"Pleasure doin' business with y'all." The man with an unmistakable Texas drawl touched the muzzle of his gun to the brim of his hat.

Daley took one last look at the pair as he gathered his lines. He didn't need a second invitation.

"Hey-up haw!" Bass watched the stage disappear down the road. He stepped down from his horse and joined Collins at the strongbox. He dropped to one knee. Neatly packed sacks of gold lined the box three layers deep.

"There must be twenty thousand here."

Collins nodded. "Yeah, sure looks pretty, don't it. Let's get it loaded and get the hell out of here."

The pair hastily filled their saddlebags. Bass stepped into the saddle. Collins's horse turned skittish, dancing in a circle as he attempted to mount. He drew a left rein, tucking the horse's muzzle to his shoulder and stepped aboard. Bass wheeled his blue roan and led them southeast at a gallop.

ONE

Denver, 1906

My name is Robert Brentwood. I am employed as a reporter for the *Denver Tribune,* though in this venture I've come to compile a record of the Great Western Detective League for a book I expect to pen one day. I stumbled on reports of this association of law enforcement officers in the *Tribune* archives. Imagine my surprise when I discovered quite by accident that the mastermind behind this storied network of crime fighters was still alive and comfortably ensconced at the Shady Grove Rest Home and Convalescent Center. My nascent writing career seemed foreordained by so fortuitous a discovery.

I arrived at Shady Grove one bright autumn afternoon. My enquiry at the reception desk was directed to a sun-washed veranda looking out over purpled peaks splashed in fall color. I found Colonel David J. Crook seated in a wheelchair soaking up the sun. He sat ramrod straight with an air that denied the ravages of his near eighty years, his only concession to the cool mountain air being a blanket wrapped about his legs. He had thick white hair, bushy muttonchops, accenting a strong jaw and stature that retained the calm, cool measure of his younger years. A creaky floorboard announced my approach. He glanced my way, his bright blue eyes alert beneath folded wrinkles and bushy brows.

"Colonel Crook?"

"I am."

"Robert Brentwood, *Denver Tribune*. I wonder if you might spare me a moment of your time?"

"Time? Time young fella, is all I got. These days all of it's spare. Pull up a chair."

I drew a nearby rocker down the porch and took a seat beside him.

"What possible interest could the *Denver Tribune* have in an old soldier like me?"

"Actually, sir it is more a personal matter, though I am a professional writer."

"All right then, what possible interest might a bright young professional writer have in an old soldier like me?"

"I'd like to talk to you about the Great Western Detective League."

He arched an eyebrow and broke into a wistful smile as if recalling an old friend. "What prompts your interest in that?"

"Some stories I found in the *Tribune* archives. I'd like to write a book about the league. I'd like to hear your side of those stories."

"A book? Well if that don't beat all. Those stories are old news."

"Not to me. You and your colleagues pioneered some very progressive criminal-investigation techniques. I think those innovations deserve recognition."

He chuckled. "Pinkerton got credit for all that."

"More than he deserved I'm sure. This is your chance to set the record straight."

He knit his brows down the bridge of his nose. "You're serious aren't you?"

"Quite serious."

He pursed his lips. "All right, where would you like to begin?"

"Would you like to go inside? You might be more comfortable there."

"Hell no! It's too warm in there. Winter'll have us cooped up in that hothouse soon enough. This time of year I take all the mountain air I can get. You get to be my age son, you never know when the time for that will run out."

I pulled a notebook and pencil from my coat pocket. Truth be told, I was thinking more about my cold fingers than the old man's comfort. I opened the notepad. "What can you tell me about Sam Bass and the Big Springs train robbery?"

His eyes drifted off up a mountain of recollection. "Briscoe Cane, Big Springs was his first case with us. First time we had a run in with Pinkerton too. The best thing to come out of that was Longstreet."

"Tell me about it."

"It all started with a stage holdup. Bass and his partner hit a Deadwood to Cheyenne stage and made off with a Wells Fargo gold shipment. Wells Fargo never took a thing like that lying down. They had a reputation to protect."

Cheyenne
1877

The Deadwood stage wheeled off the stage road, the team straining in their traces. The coach rumbled west on Sixteenth Street. "Whoa!" Charlie Tiller, the relief driver, hauled lines, drawing the stage to a halt at the station. The freshly painted sign proclaimed *Cheyenne and Black Hills Stage and Express Line.* Most folks called it the Cheyenne & Deadwood stage. The line carried prospectors and profiteers north to the Black Hills goldfields. On the return run it carried gold bound for City National Bank of Cheyenne. It took two days to make the three-hundred-mile run from Cheyenne to Deadwood with rest stops to change horses every ten miles.

Ben Munson, the stationmaster, stepped onto the boardwalk accompanied by two Wells Fargo men waiting to deliver the gold shipment to City National Bank.

Tiller looked down from the box. "Best call the sheriff, Ben. They ain't nothin' here for them two to guard. Road agents hit Pete Daley north of the forty-mile south station."

Pale morning sun fought its way through the grime coating the passenger lounge windows. It pooled on a nearly new plank floor already stained with dried mud and footprints. Straight-backed benches lined the wall facing the ticket counter. Waiting passengers sat here and there, fanning themselves against oppressive late summer heat.

Wells Fargo Agent David Dickerson mopped his brow with a linen handkerchief gone damp with the chore. He paced the lounge, impatiently waiting for Sheriff Calhoun. Losing a large shipment would not be well received in San Francisco. He expected a shipment of that size would be insured. That might mitigate the loss in financial terms, but it did little to deflect the damage done to the Wells Fargo reputation. The station door swung open filled by the sheriff's substantial silhouette. He stepped inside and closed the door. Dickerson turned on the lawman, face flushed, jowls straining his sweat-stained collar. His plump lips sputtered in frustration.

"So Sheriff, what's to be done about it?"

"Hold your horses Dickerson. Give me a minute to figure out what the hell happened here."

Charlie Tiller stood hat in hand beside the stationmaster's desk. Munson sat at his desk. He hated sitting there no more useful than teets on a bull. Then again better that than finding himself in Dickerson's shoes. The Wells Fargo man was the one with the twenty-thousand-dollar problem. Wells Fargo was his customer so he had to bear some responsibility here, but Wells Fargo was paid to provide security for these shipments. They were a passenger as far as the Cheyenne & Deadwood was concerned. The sheriff crossed the lounge to Munson's desk followed closely by the Wells Fargo man.

"All right, Ben what happened?"

Munson handed Calhoun a single sheet of paper marked and witnessed by Pete Daley. Daley was the driver at the time of the robbery. He didn't have much to offer by way of particulars. Two masked men stopped the stage two miles north of the forty-mile stop. They lifted the strongbox and sent the coach on its way.

"Not much to go on here."

Munson shook his head.

"Are you sure that's all there is?" He glanced from Munson to Tiller.

"Charlie Tiller here is the relief driver. He brought in Pete's statement," Munson said, as if to excuse Tiller.

"Did he give anyone a description?"

The sheriff turned to Tiller. The driver twisted his hat in his hands and shrugged. "Our shotgun messenger reported that one of them rode a blue roan and that one sounded like he might be a Texan," Dickerson said.

"That's it?"

"That's it, Sheriff. Sorry, best we can do," Munson said.

Calhoun scratched the stubble on his chin. "Not much to go on."

Dickerson drew up his bulk. "Twenty thousand dollars in gold is plenty to go on, Sheriff. So what's to be done?"

Calhoun pulled a scowl, growing impatient with the pushy express agent. He shrugged. "That stage was robbed two hundred and sixty miles from here. It's not my jurisdiction even if I had the manpower to go chasin' up there. Hell, it ain't even in Deadwood jurisdiction if they was to have a lawman up there, which they don't."

"So you're tellin' me there's nothing you can do about armed robbery and the loss of twenty thousand dollars in gold."

"I'm tellin' you it's outside my jurisdiction. You're the one hired to protect that shipment."

"And that's what I'm supposed to tell my superiors?"

"That's your problem, Dickerson. Not mine."

Denver
Two Days Later

"Colonel Crook?"

The feller at the office door that afternoon looked like he might be an undertaker. Course I knew he wasn't an undertaker. I knew all the undertakers in Denver. That sort of went with my line of work. He stuck out his hand with a business card.

"Samuel Fairchild, Wells Fargo."

"Mr. Fairchild, what can I do for you?"

"Wells Fargo would like to engage the services of your Great Western Detective League in a matter of vital interest."

"Vital interest is it? How may we be of service?"

"May I have a seat?"

"Please." He took a seat across the desk. I settled into my chair.

"Four days ago the Cheyenne & Deadwood stage was robbed of twenty thousand dollars in gold. The shipment was under Wells Fargo protection. We would like to engage you to recover it. We are prepared to offer you a reward of one thousand five hundred dollars for the apprehension of those responsible. We will add a one-thousand-dollar bonus for the recovery of our shipment. The terms of our offer are detailed in this engagement letter." He drew a folded page from a leather case and slid it across the desk.

I scanned the page. It was all there all right. Trouble was I didn't have an operative standing by just then to take on such an assignment. I needed to think. I opened my notebook and took up my pen.

"What can you tell me about the robbery?"

"Not much I'm afraid."

He was right about that. It took almost no time at all to recount the meager facts of the case. It was nowhere near enough time for me to devise a way to take on such a lucrative assignment. Fortunately as is true of invention, necessity can also mother inspiration. By the time I scrawled the last of my scanty notes, I had a way forward. Well I didn't exactly have a way forward. I had a way that might work. It was a bit chancy, but then few things in life are risk free. Given the size of the prize I thought I just might be able to recruit the operative I needed.

"Mr. Fairchild, the Great Western Detective League is at your service." I held up his card. "May I contact you at this office when we have something to report?"

Two

Silver Slipper Saloon

Denver

I found him seated back to the wall at a corner table in one of the more disreputable saloons in a shabby part of town. Briscoe Cane was easily recognizable from the file I'd compiled on him. He bore lean weather lined features that might have been stitched out of old saddle leather. He had hawk features, punctuated by cold gray eyes animated by some inner light that turned on and turned off with his interest. Shoulder-length hair, gray before its time, gave him an aged appearance. His lean, angular, hickory-hard frame at first appeared awkward. For the object of one of his pursuits, misestimating his appearance might prove fatal. Cane was known to possess cat-like quickness and deadly accuracy in the use of a veritable arsenal of weaponry concealed under a black frock coat. I approached his table under cover of a friendly smile.

"Mr. Cane?"

"What's it to you?"

"I'd like a word with you."

"Air's free."

"May I sit?" He favored me with an annoyed glance.

"Suit yourself."

"Mr. Cane, I've followed your work with interest. I could use a man of your abilities in my organization."

"My abilities? What do you know of my abilities? We've never met."

It was true, we had never met. But my file on the man was rather complete. "I know, for example, you favor a pair of fine-balanced bone-handled blades, one sheathed behind that .44 holster rig and the other in your left boot. I know you can draw and throw with either hand fast enough to silently defeat another man's gun draw."

He arched a brow.

"I know you are equally fast with that Colt and a .41 caliber Forehand & Wadsworth Bull Dog rigged for cross draw at your back. Some consider a spur trigger pocket pistol the weapon of choice for a whore. Such a notion would sadly misestimate your use of it. Those that do, seldom do so for long."

His eyes narrowed in a squint. "Where the hell did you get all this, Mr. ahh?"

"Crook, Colonel David J. Crook, US Army retired. Where I got the information is unimportant. What is important is that I have it. I also know you carry a Henry rifle and I'm told you can pluck out a man's eye at a thousand paces. I know that when called for, you possess a master craftsman's skills with explosives. In my humble opinion, were it not for the staunch religious foundation afforded by your upbringing you might have had a more prosperous career as an assassin than the one you have as a bounty hunter. So as you see, your abilities are quite well suited to my organization."

His brows bunched over the bridge of his nose. "Your organization?"

"Yes, the Great Western Detective League. We are an association of law enforcement professionals across the West. We cooperate in the solving of crimes."

"A law enforcement association headed by a man named Crook. Other than a bit of humor I don't see what that's got to do with me. I hunt for bounty."

"Precisely! So do we, after a fashion. And that's why you would be a perfect fit for my organization."

"I work alone."

"If you prefer, that can be arranged."

"Don't need no arrangin.' I work alone now."

"But don't you see that's your problem?"

"Look, Colonel I work alone. I don't need no organization."

"Oh but you do."

"Why?"

"For information."

"For information. What's that supposed to mean?"

"What exactly are you working on now, Mr. Cane?"

"What business is that of yours?"

"Further to my point, at the moment you're not working on anything." *I didn't know that of course. It was only a guess. Like hunches, guesses are things an investigator must play from time to time.*

He scratched the bristled stubble on his chin. "How'd you know that?"

I shrugged. "Investigators are paid to know things. Your current circumstance suits my point perfectly. You are not gainfully engaged at the moment. I on the other hand have here in my pocket a two-thousand-five-hundred-dollar opportunity."

Both brows parted wide eyed. He waved the bartender over with a glass and poured me a drink.

"Two thousand five hundred dollars you say."

"That's correct. Your share could amount to one thousand five hundred dollars if you take the assignment and succeed."

"What about the rest?"

"That belongs to the Great Western Detective League. I take twenty-five percent to compensate my administration of the league. The other fifteen percent goes into an escrow for distribution in equal shares to all league members at the end of the year. That yearly bonus can amount to a tidy sum. It assures our members' interest in the league's overall success."

"Hell if I work alone, I get the whole thing."

"No you don't. If you work alone, you sit here not working. That's the value of information. That's the value of belonging to the league. The league casts a wide net. We get the best information. We get superior results. So superior that clients like Wells Fargo seek us out with opportunities like this one." I drew a folded sheet from my inside coat pocket for emphasis. He eyed it. "Is it better to work steady for sixty percent of the proceeds plus a bonus on the success of other league members; or to sit here idle for one hundred percent of sometimes?" His mouth turned down at the corners, bent in serious contemplation.

"All right, Colonel, I'll give your league a try. Tell me about this opportunity of yours."

"Splendid!"

Stage Road to Deadwood

Cane caught a stage north to Cheyenne the next morning. By his estimation wherever the bandits went, they had a six-day head start. That lead would only get bigger by the time he got to see if he could find anything amounting to a trail at the scene of the holdup. He caught the northbound Cheyenne & Deadwood stage the following day. He pretty much kept to himself with his two fellow passengers. One a drummer in a shabby suit with a fondness for a bottle he kept in his coat pocket. The other a working girl migrating north to the mining opportunities in Deadwood. The drummer made no secret of his ogling interest in the dove's breasts. She affected disinterest for the moment. Cane expected that to change at the first opportunity to relieve the man of some coin.

A day and a half out of Cheyenne the stage rocked along the

dusty road approaching the two-hundred-sixty-mile rest stop. This would be the end of the line for Cane. According to the report Crook gave him, the holdup occurred two miles north of this stop. He meant to inspect the crime scene and let his observations there decide his next move.

He'd had a brief conversation with the relief driver who took over at the two-hundred-mile station. By a stroke of good fortune, Pete Daley was the driver the day of the holdup. He planned to finish that conversation before he left the stage.

He felt the team slow. He stuck his head out the window, catching a brief glimpse of the station before pulling back from the choking dust clouds. The road descended gently toward the station at the bottom of a shallow valley. The rough cut log structure had a privy and corral, much like the others they'd passed. This was one of the larger stations with a small passenger lounge where meals were served. These were spaced along the route between smaller stations that provided fresh horses but few comforts. The larger stations had a two-man crew to handle the horses and the cooking.

"Whoa!" Daley hauled lines, drawing his team to a lurching halt beside the station. He set the brake and climbed down from the box. He opened the coach door.

"Thirty-minute stop, folks."

Cane stepped down and offered a hand to the dove. She took it, favoring him with a smile that said if he were interested she'd be more than pleased to forego the drummer's favors. He returned her smile expecting she'd get her piece of the drummer's poke about as soon as he left the two of them to the coach seats. The drummer stepped down and followed the sway of her hips up the steps to the passenger lounge. Hell, Cane thought, she might have it all by the time they covered the last forty miles to Deadwood.

Dust devils swirled across the corral, dancing among horses

sleeping hip-shot, noses turned to the breeze. A wiry old codger rounded the corner from behind the station. A wind-whipped bush of gray whiskers and greasy shoulder-length hair flapping wildly under a dusty slouch hat.

"Hey, Pete, we'll have a fresh team hitched up for you in no time."

"Thanks, Jake," the driver said.

"Can I have a word, Pete?"

"Sure, Cane. What is it?"

"I'd like some information about the holdup last week."

"Sure. Much as I got, which ain't much. You the law?"

"After a fashion. Great Western Detective League. Wells Fargo retained us to look into the matter."

"Private law, makes sense out here. There ain't no other law."

"That's it."

"Come on, let's catch a cup of the mud Cookie calls coffee."

The gangly gaited driver led the way to the station. He clumped up the plank steps into a dimly lit passenger lounge with a rough-cut table and benches. Cane guessed the benches were intended to help the passengers appreciate the thinly padded coach seats.

"Have a seat," Daley said. "Cookie bring us some of that sludge you call coffee." The sound of tin cups rattled from the kitchen, one of two rooms adjoining the lounge.

Cookie appeared carrying a steaming pot and tin cups. Heavyset and grizzly he looked like he might be his best customer. A badly stained apron strained at his girth over the sweat-soiled top of his union suit. He grunted what passed for a greeting and poured two steaming cups of coffee, set down the pot and waddled back to the kitchen.

Daley cocked his head in the direction of his retreating bulk. "None too sociable, but not a half bad cook. Now what can I do for you?"

"What can you tell me about the holdup?"

"Not much I'm afraid. They hit us a couple of miles north of here. The southbound run climbs a long rise into a blind curve. The team's mostly played out by the time you get there. Between that and the climb you come into that curve at a walk. Two of 'em blocked the road with their guns drawn."

"What did they look like?"

He shrugged. "Both of 'em was masked up. The taller one spoke with an accent I took for Texan. He rode a blue roan. Not much to the other one other than the nasty way he threw that gun around. You seen one trail-dusted hombre on a bay horse, you seen 'em all."

"What happened?"

"The big one called for the box. The Wells Fargo messenger threw it down. The other guy shot off the lock, took a look at the haul and sent us on our way. Didn't have to ask twice as far as I was concerned."

"That's it?"

"That's it. Sorry I couldn't be more help."

"I could use one more thing."

"What's that?"

"See if you can get your stationmaster to loan me the use of a horse for a couple of hours. I'd like to look around up there to see if I can pick up any sign of which way they went."

Ten minutes later the stage pulled out trailing a spare horse tacked up with Cane's saddle. Two miles up the road Daley hauled lines in a narrow gulch that entered a blind curve to the north.

"This is it," he called.

Cane tipped his hat to the dove and climbed out of the coach. He untied the spare horse and glanced up at Daley.

"Much obliged."

"Good luck. I hope you get the sons a bitches, though by

now I expect they're long gone as smoke."

"Likely so. Again much obliged."

"Hey-up haw!"

The stage rumbled around the bend out of sight save a trailing dun cloud. Cane walked the site. You couldn't ask for a better place to rob a stage. That part was easy. The question was what happened afterward? Which way did the outlaws go? If they took the stage road north or south, picking up a trail would be all but impossible. He looked around. The gulch hemmed in the road on both sides. He noticed a stone that looked out of place beside the road. He bent down to examine it. Of course it didn't belong there. A chunk of metal wasn't a stone. He picked up a piece of the blown padlock and turned it over in his hand. Yup, they'd opened the strongbox all right. He tossed the lock aside and stood.

Where did two men go with twenty thousand in gold? Where did they go to enjoy it? Deadwood said north. No law up there either. The nearest law was two hundred sixty miles south. That made for another reason to go north. Everything pointed to Deadwood, everything except two things. A couple of men spending a good time's worth of gold might get noticed in a place like Deadwood that had just taken a big loss. A man might also go south if he was to do the least expected thing. If they were to send a posse out of Cheyenne, heading south would have the effect of doubling back on them. If you stayed off the stage road and didn't run smack into them, you could put a lot of miles behind them before they figured out what happened, if they ever did figure it out.

His eyes followed the stage road back south. He noticed a break in the rocks along the east wall. He led his horse to the opening and ground tied him. Horse sign said someone had waited here. They'd waited for the stage here out of sight. Cheyenne lay off to the southwest. If it was him, what would he do? Southeast, he'd double back southeast. He collected his horse, toed a stirrup and swung down the road far enough to clear the gulch wall and left the road southeast in a lazy circle.

Within a half hour he crossed a faint sign. He drew rein and stepped down. He prowled around a partial print, then two, then another. It wasn't a trail a man could follow. No one could bank on a week-old trail that might lead a hundred fifty miles from here and more. That said, this trail had to be the bandits'. Anyone else headed south would follow the stage road. Why wouldn't you, unless you were avoiding detection? They were headed south by southeast. He wasn't about to catch them by following this trail that far. Where would two men with twenty thousand dollars in gold go? That was the question. He smiled. He had a couple of days to think that one through.

He boarded the Cheyenne & Deadwood southbound the next day for the two-day run back to Cheyenne. He'd cover two hundred sixty miles in a day and a half. He reckoned it the fastest way to make up ground on the men he was after. He'd find them east of Cheyenne, somewhere east, but where?

Shady Grove

The colonel paused. His head nodded. I put down my pad and pencil. An attendant appeared at my side. She was dressed in a pale blue dress with a clean white apron. The soft form of a woman's figure could not be denied by the severity of her uniform. She had a kind face, pert lips and short curled black hair crowned by a nurse's cap. Her eyes were as soft as melted chocolates filled with caramel. She nodded to the colonel.

"I believe he's ready for his nap."

She sounded as soft as her caramel eyes. The colonel glanced awake.

"She's come to take me away. It's the only good part of goin'."

She blushed.

"Tomorrow's Saturday, young feller. If you've nothing better to do, come back and I'll tell you more of the story."

"I'd like that," I said. I couldn't help a glance at the girl. She smiled a smile fit to give the Mona Lisa mirth. "One more question before I go if I may. Do you mean to tell me that Cane deduced a week-old trail out of the robbery scene?"

His eyes crinkled. "I knew a lot about Briscoe Cane when I hired him. There was a lot I didn't know. The man saw things. He sensed things. I swear he could follow a fart in a snowstorm." Mona Lisa blushed.

"That and he had an uncanny capacity for devious thinking. You'll see."

She wheeled him away. I watched them go. Well to be honest, I watched her hips.

I presented myself at the reception desk the following morning. I was told to meet the colonel out on the veranda. It seemed we would spend another day in the crisp fall air. I waited, soaking up as much warmth as the sunshine promised. My fingers reddened with the chill. Mona Lisa wheeled him out to his place in the sun. I'll admit I forgot about the cold. She smiled. I must have too. The colonel looked me up and down.

"Came back for more I see."

"Good morning, Colonel. I did."

"I suppose you'll want to hear more of the story in the bargain."

"Why yes, of course. That's the point."

"Is it?"

THREE

Sydney, Nebraska

Sydney made a rough and tumble base camp on the gold road to Deadwood. It sprang up to provision miners hoping to find their fortune in the Black Hills. It flourished under the protection of Camp Robinson, the army post charged with protecting the passage to Deadwood. Hostile Indians had mostly been driven north after the Custer massacre. The army presence intended to remind any that might forget that the treaty giving the tribes the Black Hills had been broken.

The town was little more than a collection of tent tops and log construction. Valentine's General Store and a small blacksmith shop were the only finished structures. A hand-lettered sign beside the largest tent top proclaimed *Last Stop Saloon*. Jake McCoy, the proprietor, intended to name the place Last Stop Before Prosperity, but he couldn't find a signboard of suitable size for such an auspicious name. It didn't matter. The Last Stop had whiskey, gambling and whore cribs next door.

The evening crowd made a raucous din even with the tent sides rolled up on a pleasant evening. Kerosene lanterns hung on ropes strung between the tent poles created islands of light over the shadowy crowd. Oily black smoke, mingled with clouds of tobacco smoke trapped under the canvas top, stained the fabric a yellowish gray. A piano man in a misshapen bowler plunked out an indistinct tune that gave the place a ring familiar to saloons from Saint Louis to Sacramento.

Bass and Collins sat at a corner table in the company of three tough-cut characters, Tom Nixon, Bill Heffridge and Jim Berry. Bass had a passing acquaintance with Nixon and knew him for the sort that might come in handy for the job he had on his mind. One he and Collins couldn't pull off alone. He invited them for a drink.

"So Tom, where you boys headed?"

"Up Deadwood way."

"Taken to the gold business?"

"Not diggin' if that's what you mean."

"I didn't think so. You may be thinkin' about the Cheyenne & Deadwood stage."

Nixon nodded.

"Joel here and me know some about the Cheyenne & Deadwood stage."

"Do tell." Nixon seemed to be the leader. He was more interested in Bass's offer of a drink than his opinion of the stage business.

"If you boys is thinkin' about that bit of gold business, I gotta tell you there's better ways to play the game. Joel and I been up there. Things is, shall we say, crowded. You not only gotta contend with guards on the shipment, you gotta deal with other gangs beatin' you to the take or shootin' you up for gettin' to it first."

Nixon tossed his drink and poured another. "So if pickin's up there is poor and troublesome, I 'spect you got a better idea."

"I tell you boys, if we get this right it'll be bigger than clean-in' out most any bank in the territory."

Nixon smoothed his mustache in the web between his thumb and forefinger. "Yeah? All right you got our attention. What's the play?"

"Eastbound shipments out of the San Francisco mint roll by train."

Nixon's eyes narrowed. He leaned into the scarred tabletop, with Heffridge and Berry at each elbow. "You plannin' on hittin' a train?"

"Damn right."

Berry tilted his chin toward Bass, a shadow of doubt in his eye. "How you gonna know which train's carryin' a shipment?"

"I got a way. I'm workin' on it now."

Heffridge aimed a stream of tobacco juice at a nearby spittoon. Bass hoped he was a better shot with a gun. He shifted the chew to his right cheek.

"What kinda guard they put on a shipment like that?"

"Not as big as you'd think and not near big enough where we're concerned."

Nixon knocked back his drink and elbowed Heffridge for the bottle. He poured another and passed it to Berry. "When you figure you'll be ready?"

"That depends on the shipping schedule. I should know in a day or two."

Berry knit his bushy brows. "Where you fixin' to hit this train?"

"At a two o'clock in the morning watering station. You boys got all the information you need. You in or out?"

Nixon sat back. He glanced from Berry to Heffridge. He cut his eyes back to Bass. "We're in."

Bass ambled down to the depot in the gloom gathering around early evening. Prairie wind threw a bouncing sage ball across the tracks as he climbed the deserted platform. The next train wasn't due for three hours. He stepped into the passenger lounge. A rumpled bundle in a wool coat and britches stretched out snoring softly on a wooden bench. A second man sat beneath a sputtering oil lamp reading a thumb-worn Bible. Bass checked the schedule board long enough for his contact to notice him. He went back out to the platform, sidled down to the end and leaned against the wall to wait.

Several minutes later the depot door opened. A slight silhouette appeared in the lighted doorway and disappeared with the closing. The contact glanced around until he located Bass. He shuffled down the platform. Little could be made of his features save the glare of low light on his spectacles and a shine on his bald pate. He paused beside Bass his eyes darting nervously.

"Have you got it?"

His head bobbed. "You have what we agreed?"

Bass released a stack of twenty-dollar gold pieces, letting them clatter from one hand to the other in reply.

The contact held out his hand.

"You first."

"The two fifteen out of San Francisco on the eighteenth."

"You're sure?"

"Sure as the Union Pacific schedule."

Bass let ten twenty-dollar gold pieces clatter into the telegrapher's outstretched hand.

Nebraska

Two days east of Cheyenne Cane struck a creek. It meandered out of the northwest slow and muddy, winding its way southeast through rolling hills of prairie grass burnished golden brown by the late-summer sun. He drew rein and let his long striding gray gelding Smoke have his head to drink. *Water.* If they passed this way they'd stop at least to water the horses, maybe even camp. It fit the general direction he figured they were on. This was one of those cases where either he was right, or it didn't matter. Smoke lifted his head and blew his nose. He reckoned to follow the stream as long as it suited his purpose. He couldn't be any more wrong and maybe, just maybe he'd catch a break.

Hours passed through midday. The streambed showed no trail sign. As the sun began to sink toward the western horizon he spotted a place along the north bank. Stone gathered to bed a fire. He drew rein and stepped down to examine the bank. His boots crunched the stony bank as he examined the site. Sunlight glittered yellow on the surface of muddy water.

The sound was more hiss than rattle, though instantly recognizable for the jolt that grabbed a man's gut on hearing it. Smoke bolted. The frightened animal shrieked, reared and backed up the bank pawing the air, its nostrils flared.

The snake coiled on the rocky bank, too close to rule out a strike. Cane froze. The snake's eyes glittered. Its tongue flicked at the air tasting the scent of him. As luck had it, his body blocked the snake's view of his right hand. He eased it up to the Bull Dog's smooth ivory grips. He eased the hammer back, estimating the distance the snake might reach in a strike. He drew, stepped back and fired in one lightning-like motion. His shot missed the rattling coil, exploding in a sharp spray of stone chips. The snake lashed out, falling just short of his boot. He fired again. The shot nicked a long diamond marking behind the head. The snake recoiled. A third shot cut the coiled mass in half. Powder smoke drifted away. He let out his breath with it.

That was close. He holstered his gun. Smoke stood up the creek bank, ears pulled back, eyes wide, nostrils flared, his powerful chest heaving. Cane started toward the terrified animal slowly. "Easy now." The gray tossed his head and stomped nervously. A quiver of tension rippled his withers. Cane stroked his neck, gentling his nerves as he gathered his reins. He led him back down to the creek and let him settle. When the horse was quietly cropping river grass, he left him and circled the area around the fire sign.

It was a campsite all right. He found sign of one or two horses hobbled to graze. The sign he read to be a week or more old. That could be about right. If this was their trail where did they go from here? He waded across the creek and walked the south bank. A faint trail of crushed sage and partial hoofprints whispered a southerly direction. Nothing new, though it served to agree with his working deduction. Where do two men with pockets full of gold go from here? He'd posed that question before. This time his working theory suggested an answer. By his reckoning he was a day's ride from Sydney, Nebraska. Sydney was an established stop on the gold road to Deadwood. It made sense. Just the sort of town a man with money might go to have a good time.

He pitched camp and spent the night, growing a powerful hunch he was on the right track. Next morning he toed a stirrup, swung into the saddle and nudged Smoke into the stream. At the far bank he eased him south.

Julesburg, Colorado

Julesburg sat on the north bank of the South Platte River, south of the Union Pacific rail line. A dilapidated depot, platform, privy and watering station made up the last comfort stop before the roll into Cheyenne. The town consisted of a ramshackle collection of adobe houses, a stable, stores and saloons. Once an end-of-track boomtown on the road to Denver, Julesburg missed its ticket to wealth and prosperity when Grenville Dodge took the Union Pacific line north to Cheyenne. A Denver spur and a small stockyard, serving western Nebraska and northeastern Colorado, eventually provided some commercial enterprise, though little more than a hollow echo of the once great promise.

Bass, Collins and the boys rode out of a shimmering expanse of Nebraska plain on a hot dusty afternoon. Bass drew rein northwest of the depot. Prairie wind whipped out of the west, hurling sage balls before it chased by sheets of sand and dust.

Heffridge spat a stream of tobacco juice into the dried sage at his horse's hoof. Berry wiped his parched lips with the back of his hand. He unfastened the canteen tied to the cantle of his saddle, pulled the cork and took a swallow.

Nixon slacked his reins, resting a gloved hand on the saddle horn. "Sure don't look like much."

Bass's blue roan stomped and shifted hip-shot. "That's the point. This here's the nearest town and there ain't no law. The nearest law's in Cheyenne. We'll hit that train and be long gone before anybody knows what happened." He squeezed up a jog toward the west end of town.

He pulled them down to a walk as they approached the depot, preparing to cross the tracks. The depot looked to be a one-room, rough-cut log construction. A plank platform ran along the building trackside. The watering station with its rusted filling trough stood west of the depot, deserted stock pens and loading chutes stood off to the east. A careful observer might have recognized the dark-eyed stranger's interest in the depot for something more than casual. No one did.

Up close Julesburg looked more threadbare than it had from a distance. The few log and rough-cut wood buildings scattered among the adobe offered a spectacle of disrepair. A paint drummer might have done a good business in town if there were any cash money for such purposes. Bass drew rein at the hitch rack out front of the first saloon they came to. A badly weathered hand-lettered sign proclaimed it the Rusty Spike. Somebody had a sense of humor. He stepped down.

"Joel, you and Heffridge head over to that general store yonder." He pointed down the block and across the dusty ruts that passed for a street. "We're gonna need trail supplies when this is over. We'll be splittin' up so buy sharp. Meet us back here when you're done."

Collins started to protest. Why should he have to wait his thirst on something the new men could do? A second look from Bass put up the thought. Things were testy with him since Deadwood. He looped a rein over the splintered rack rail and stalked off down the street, trailing the lumbering Heffridge behind.

Bass clumped the boardwalk, followed by Nixon and Berry. Inside he paused to let his eyes adjust to the dim light able to make its way through the dirt-streaked windows. Familiar smells of stale beer, tobacco smoke and sawdust resolved into a thirst. He headed for a corner table, signaling the bartender in a soiled apron for a bottle and glasses. Chairs scraped rough floor planks. Burns from carelessly placed smokes scarred the cracked tabletop. The bartender arrived with a bottle and glasses. Bass tossed an eagle on the table. "We're expectin' a couple more." The bartender scooped up the coin and left them.

Nixon poured. He picked up his glass. His eyes cut to Bass. "So how do you see it?"

"Pretty simple I reckon. We ride out to Big Springs and take over the station an hour or so before she's due in. One of us replaces the stationmaster. That way we get close enough to get a drop on the engineer. The shipment will be in the mail car."

"What about guards?"

Bass shrugged. "Pinkerton, two of 'em most likely. They'll take a privy break. We take out the first one and jump the second in the mail car."

"So far no noise if we're lucky."

"Likely they ship in a safe or strongbox. Cain't help the noise for that. Afterward we divide the gold and split up. We use the river to cover our tracks."

"You got it all figured out, ain't ya Bass?"

"Best I can."

"Well it sounds pretty good. I hope you're right."

FOUR

Sydney, Nebraska

Cane rode into Sydney by the gray light of early evening. His slicker dripped rain from a storm that rolled through trailing a heavy down quilt of gray cloud. Smoke's hooves made sucking sounds as they jogged up the muddy street. The smell of mud and wet canvas mingled with the scent of rain. He only had partial prints coming out of that stream and precious little sign after that. If, in fact, the trail of the men he was after led here, he'd made it by little more than a hunch. He eyed the muddy collection of hasty construction, tent top saloons and cribs belonging to ladies for hire. Sydney sure enough had the look of a hospitable haunt for a man after a good time. Well, he was here. No time like the present to start looking.

He followed the sound of a piano to a large tent top with *Last Stop* splashed across a hand-lettered signboard. A picket line of stout rope strung between two scrub oak served for a hitch rack. He stepped down and looped Smoke's rein over the line. He inspected the stock tied there. No sign of a blue roan. Then again that was probably too much to hope for. He slogged through the mud to a plank walk that led to an open-air saloon. The planks had the look of being thrown down in honor of the rain.

Inside a sparse crowd stood along the Last Stop rail. A couple of early games were open for business. The real action wouldn't get going until later. A quick look at the crowd didn't reveal any obvious suspects. He found his way to the bar. The bartender wandered over, polishing a glass.

"What'll it be?"

"Whiskey."

The bartender set down a glass and poured. "You want me to leave the bottle?"

Cane nodded. "I'm lookin' for a couple of men."

"We see a lot of 'em, most everyone on their way to Dead-wood."

"These two would be comin' from Deadwood."

"Don't see so many of those. Them that do come back is mostly broke."

"These two are well-heeled in gold. One's tall, talks with an accent, likely a Texan. He rides a blue roan. The other's a smaller fella, got plenty of attitude."

The bartender shook his head. "Cain't say as I recall anyone like that."

"I think I know who you mean." The speaker directed a stream of tobacco juice into a brass spittoon at his boot. The man wore mud-stained wool britches, a rumpled coat and shapeless crown hat. He had watery blue eyes and a bush of unkempt red whiskers. "I only noticed 'em cause I was havin' a drink with Jim Berry, Bill Heffridge and Tom Nixon when the tall one started talkin' to Tom."

"Briscoe Cane's the name." He stuck out his hand.

The man clasped it in a meaty paw. "Simon Purdy."

"I'd be pleased to buy you a drink Mr. Purdy."

"You buy me a drink, you best call me Simon." He passed his glass along the bar.

Cane poured. He lifted his glass. "Pleased to meet you, Simon. Call me Briscoe."

Purdy lifted his glass and took a swallow.

"Mind tellin' me what happened with your friends and those men?"

Purdy shrugged. "Nixon and Heffridge was talkin' about some kind of business scheme like they was always doin'."

"What sort of business?"

Purdy scowled. "You the law?"

"Not exactly."

"Not exactly. What the hell is that supposed to mean?"

"Let's just say I'm interested in certain kinds of business. If you've got information that suits my interest, it might be worth your while." He drew a twenty-dollar gold piece from his pocket and set it on the bar.

"Hmm. No skin off my nose then. Nixon and Heffridge was talkin' about something to do with the Cheyenne & Deadwood stage."

Cane arched a brow. "The Cheyenne & Deadwood stage, you're sure?"

Purdy nodded.

"I'm interested."

"The tall one seemed to know Nixon. He walks up says hello and they start talkin'."

"Did you catch a name?"

Purdy scratched his chin. Cane topped up his glass.

"Bass, that was it. He said his name was Bass, Sam Bass. Introduced his partner as somethin' Collins. I didn't get it all."

"Then what happened?"

"Next thing you know Nixon rounds up Heffridge and Jim and the lot of 'em go off to a table."

"What happened after that?"

Purdy shrugged. "All I know is that when they broke up to leave, Jim stopped to say good-bye."

"Did he say where they were goin'?"

"He mentioned somethin' about meetin' a train."

A train. Cane tossed off his drink. "You've been a big help Simon." He slid the twenty-dollar gold piece down the bar and left.

Shady Grove

A week later I found myself once again sitting on the sun-soaked veranda, waiting for Colonel Crook. It was another one of those autumn days when the sun promises warm and the mountain air says cold. I couldn't believe we were going to sit out here for another afternoon. Mona Lisa wheeled him out the double doors from the warm reception room and down the expansive porch to where I sat, hoping to warm myself in the sun. Once again I forgot the chill. *How does a woman look that good wearing a drab institutional uniform?* I found myself at a loss, though not necessarily over that particular question. She smiled that smile of hers, the tip of her nose pink with the cold.

"Good afternoon, Colonel."

"Robert, I'm surprised you'd subject yourself to another of my nostalgic ramblings."

"How could I not?"

Our eyes met.

"You haven't finished the story."

She turned to go. I'm afraid my attention wandered after her.

"Yes, I see that. She's a lovely girl. Penny I think they call her. You should introduce yourself."

I came back to the purpose at hand. Colonel Crook had a twinkle in his eye.

"Now where were we?"

I consulted my notes. "Cane just discovered the men he was following were Sam Bass and a man named Collins."

"Ah yes, Joel Collins."

"According to the *Tribune* archives, Sam Bass was quite the notorious outlaw in his day."

"He was a bad one all right, only most of that came later. These events occurred early in his outlaw career."

"Continue then, please."

"You're sure you don't want to take a few moments to track down that young lady and introduce yourself?"

I reddened. I hoped he didn't notice for the cold. "Please, continue."

Big Springs, Nebraska
September 18

Bass drew rein on a low rise overlooking a ragged scar beside the rail line a half mile distant. A watering station and small depot were about all that remained from the days when a tent top town boomed at end-of-track. That town, like so many others along the right-of-way, picked up with the crews and moved on to the next stop. What remained served the purposes of a watering stop for man and machine.

Bass wheeled his horse and backtracked off the rise. He circled north concealed by a ridgeline to a grassy notch behind the depot. He drew a halt and stepped down. "Picket the horses and get some rest. I'm goin' up top to have a look around."

A brisk west wind tossed the grassy draw as Bass climbed to the top of the ridge. He lay on his belly, looking through the sweet-smelling grass at the rough-cut depot below. A small platform extended out to the track. The privy stood behind the west end of the depot. An overgrown rutted roadway ran along the south side of the tracks, past the abandoned remnants of a town. A lonely dust devil swirled down the street pushed along by the wind. The ramshackle hulk of a livery stable and blacksmith shop stood across the road from the depot beside a small corral with a broken rail. A single hip-shot horse slept nose to the wind, the only sign of life in sight.

A portly stationmaster came around the shadow of the east

wall and ambled toward the privy. Sun glinted off his bald pate. He wore a white shirt with garters at the sleeves. He disappeared into the small one-holer. Bass doubted the station had any more crew than him or maybe one more. A telegraph wire stretched to the station from a trackside pole. He made a mental note to cut it. The privy door opened and the stationmaster emerged into the sunlight buttoning his britches. He didn't appear to be armed. Bass half smiled. It looked like a piece of cake. His palms itched at the prospect of all that money.

FIVE

September 19

One o'clock. Bass snapped his watchcase closed. "Come on boys time to rise and shine." He hoisted his saddle over his shoulder. The men began to rouse themselves. He gave the snoring Heffridge a nudge with his boot as he passed on his way to the picket line.

The horses began to stir, sensing night work as he reached them. He settled the blanket on the back of his roan and hoisted the saddle up. Satisfied with the fit at the withers, he lifted the stirrup fender over the seat and fished the cinch from under the horse's belly. He double looped the strap through cinch and saddle rings, tugged it finger snug and tied it off. He dropped the stirrup back into place and swept his eyes around the boys.

Impatient, he stepped into the saddle to hurry them along. One by one Collins, Nixon and Berry mounted up. "Heffridge, the train will be in Buffalo Station before you get that horse saddled. Catch up when you can." He wheeled his horse and squeezed a lope up the ridge toward the depot. Heffridge scrambled into the saddle and galloped off after the sound of retreating horses.

Bass eased them down the face of the ridge. Rumpled clouds hinted at moonlight, thick and dark here, thin and gray there. The depot resolved into a black block rising up from the plain. Dim yellow light winked behind a solitary window. He led the way south toward the back of the depot and drew rein a hundred yards short of the depot. A silvered ribbon of track appeared in the west and disappeared out of sight in the east. The livery across the road lay dark and still beside its skeleton corral. Bass stepped down. Collins and the boys ground tied their horses and gathered around. He flicked the cover of his watch. *One thirty.*

"Joel, you and Berry take out the stationmaster. Be quick and keep it quiet." He cut his eyes west at a distant rumble of thunder. "Wait for the train in the depot. When she pulls in, Joel you play stationmaster and get the drop on the engineer and fireman. Berry, you keep an eye on the mail car. The Pinkertons will go to the privy by turns. Nixon you wait for the first guard by the privy. Take him out quiet. Join up at the mail car when he's down. Berry and I will take the mail car after the guard leaves. Heffridge you bring up the horses when you see Nixon head for the train. Leave us our horses and then take Joel's up to the engine. There's a lone tree north of the tracks a half mile east of the depot. We'll meet the two of you there once we get the gold loaded. He looked from one man to the next. "Any questions?" Heads shook all around. "Good. OK Joel get started, and remember, no gunplay."

Collins nodded. Thunder rumbled in the distance as the wind picked up. "Looks like you boys waitin' outside might get some wet." They went to their horses and pulled on slickers.

Collins and Berry dissolved into the night. They paused at the depot window. Collins peeked inside. The stationmaster sat at his desk. His chin rested on the rhythmic rise and fall of his chest. He ducked below the window light and turned to Barry, signaling quiet with a forefinger. "He's asleep." He masked up and drew his .44. Berry took his lead and followed up the platform.

Rolling thunder covered the soft scrape of boots on the plank platform. Collins cut his eyes to Berry at the door. Berry nodded. Collins burst through the door, his gun leveled at the startled stationmaster. The large man's eyes bulged above fleshy cheeks and jowls. He raised his arms, blinking owlishly. "I ain't no hero, don't get paid for it."

Collins motioned for Berry to tie him up. He tied the frightened man to his chair and gagged him with a spare bandanna. Outside the first splashes of rain spattered the platform and slapped the station roof. Collins trimmed the lamp wick in the window and brought the light back up.

Bass watched the lamp go dim and bright as rain pattered his hat brim. "Looks like Joel and Berry got the station under control." He covered his watch with his slicker and flicked the lid open. One *forty.*

"Best go have a look at the privy, Nixon."

"Maybe I'll take a shit to get out of this rain."

"Suit yourself. Just have your ass out of there before the Pinkerton comes callin'. I'm goin' down the line a bit to wait."

Bass left Heffridge with the horses. He followed Nixon toward the back of the depot. He climbed the platform and crossed to the east end. He drew his Colt, held it by the barrel and hooked the butt over the telegraph wire. He jerked the connection free. The wire recoiled to the base of the trackside pole. Satisfied he climbed down from the platform and walked west parallel to the tracks and far enough away to avoid being exposed by the engine headlamp.

White lightning shattered the darkness, turning the landscape into a momentary tapestry of shadow and light. Thunder rumbled through his gut. Rain slanted across the depot platform in wind whipped sheets, lashing his slicker with the furry of the storm. Off to the west a train whistled faint protest. Bass turned his back to the sharp needles of rain and checked his watch in the next flash of lightning. *Five minutes to two, it won't be long now.*

Horses whickered and pranced wide-eyed in lightning flashes. Heffridge gathered the leads, talking softly to quiet them. They could ill afford to have them bolt, leaving them stranded at the scene of a train robbery.

The whistle sounded again, closer this time. Deep in the darkness down the tracks to the west a pinpoint of light pierced the veil of rain running off Bass's hat brim. Lightning exploded again, close enough to shake the ground with an instantaneous crash of thunder. Instinctively he recoiled against the scant shelter of a lone tree. The angry edge of the storm swept past, taking the strongest winds with it and leaving a heavy downpour in its wake.

Further west lightning flashed over a gray plume belching through the concussion that followed. The headlamp danced over the roadbed, lighting rain-slicked silver rails in an eerie glow. The light grew larger as the train approached. Clouds of smoke curled from her stack bleached gray against the storm-blackened sky. The locomotive slowed behind a warning whistle blast. Brakes screeched steel on steel, white steam billowed in clouds as driving arms pushed past Bass. Up the track the engine drew level with the depot and rolled to a stop at the watering station, venting its final bursts of steam.

The depot door opened, spilling yellow light on the rain-soaked platform. Collins stepped into the pool of light, his rain slicker silhouetted briefly as he closed the station door. He held the stationmaster's lantern in front of him and made his way up the platform toward the watering station. He kept his head down against the wind and rain, his hat shielding his mask. His free hand, stuffed in his slicker pocket, held his drawn gun.

One car forward of the caboose at the west end of the platform, the mail car door cracked open. The pale glow of lamplight illuminated the dim interior. The dark silhouette of a heavyset man wearing a suit and bowler appeared in the doorway. He stepped onto the platform and hurried through the rain toward the privy at the back of the depot.

Bass masked up and drew his gun. He made his way cautiously past the caboose and climbed the platform to the mail car. The moment the Pinkerton disappeared from the platform, a second figure stepped out of the depot. The masked shadow made its way swiftly and silently across the platform to the mail car.

"Evenin'." The engineer in the grease-streaked coveralls greeted the stationmaster. The hat behind the lantern turned up, dark eyes glittered above the bandanna masking the man's other features. The dark bore of a .44 with its lethal halo of chambers appeared beside the lantern.

"Step away from the throttle. You fireman, step out here where I can see you. Nobody move and nobody gets hurt."

The Pinkerton stepped off the platform into the shadows at the back of the depot. The pressure to relieve himself fixed his attention on the black shape of the privy he could barely make out through the gloom. The gun-butt blow that caved in the back of his bowler felled him like a dead tree.

Nixon pulled the guard's pistol from his coat pocket. He used the handcuffs he found in another pocket to fasten the man's hands behind his back. Satisfied, he turned to the train. His boots splashed through muddy puddles on the path to the platform.

Bass met Berry's eyes across the dimly lit mail car doorway. He nodded. Both men stepped through the car door, guns leveled at the startled Pinkerton guard.

"Hands up!" The bandanna covering Bass's face puffed the words. The guard raised his hands, favoring the bandits with his

50

most menacing if meaningless scowl.

"Get his gun." Berry lifted a .38 from a shoulder holster inside the guard's tweed jacket.

"He'll be carryin' handcuffs. Use 'em on him." Bass turned to the strongbox. Berry found the Pinkerton's handcuffs and cuffed his hands behind his back.

"Where's the key?" The Pinkerton drew a sullen expression. "I said where's the key?" Bass cocked his gun to make the point for him.

"They don't send one with a shipment like this. The only one who might need it is the likes of you."

Heffridge watched Nixon climb the station platform framed in the dim light from the open mail car. He collected the horses and led them toward the train past the Pinkerton fallen in the muddy runnels beside the privy.

Nixon pulled up short at the corner of the depot as a dark figure climbed down from the back of the caboose. He wore a distinctive conductor's coat and hat. Rain glinted off the dull metal barrels of a sawed-off shotgun. He stepped up the platform to the mail car.

The pistol shot exploded in the close confines of the mail car. The lock on the strongbox shattered. A cloud of choking blue smoke hazed the lantern light. Bass kicked the lid off the box with the toe of his boot. The lid clattered to the worn floorboards.

Nixon's pistol spit fire from his position beside the depot. The conductor staggered. His shotgun loosed a double charge spattering the rail bed and station platform with shot. The trainman toppled to the platform.

The horses spooked, rearing wide-eyed and backing away from the gunfire. Heffridge fell to his knees in the mud, hanging on to the reins as the frightened animals dragged him through the mud.

Nixon crossed the platform. "Whoa there, easy, easy," he said to calm the horses. Gunplay was bad enough, lose the horses and they'd be in trouble. He stepped off the platform beside his own mount, catching the reins just below the bit. "Easy there." He stroked the horse's neck. Heffridge recovered his feet. The horses began to settle beside Nixon's mount. "Come on Bill, let's get these horses to the train."

"Hurry up." Bass waved at Nixon from the mail car door. "What the hell was all the shootin' for?"

Nixon tossed a shower of rain off the brim of his hat in the direction of the body lying beside the caboose. "The conductor decided to play hero."

Bass paid no attention. "Give me them saddlebags."

Nixon jerked the saddlebags from his horse and the two he led. He handed them up to Bass. "Bill take Collins's horse up to the engine. We should be ready to ride pretty quick." Heffridge set off at a trot leading Collins's bay.

Inside the car, Bass and Berry made quick work of stuffing the contents of the strongbox into the saddlebags. "Let's get the hell out of here." Bass jumped to the platform and headed for Nixon and the horses. He handed one heavily loaded saddlebag to Nixon and stepped off the platform into his saddle. Berry followed his lead. They spun their horses north and galloped behind the depot, wheeling east.

Heffridge pulled up beside the locomotive long enough for Collins to swing aboard his horse. Collins wheeled his horse east and squeezed up a lope along the roadbed. As they passed the engine he glimpsed a lantern bobbing in the darkness across the road south of the depot. He spurred up a gallop down the tracks as a muzzle flashed futile fire at their escape.

★ ★ ★ ★ ★

A lone tree stood sentinel at the east end of the old town. Bass drew rein and stepped down. "Get them saddlebags down. We'll divide up our shares here and split up." They emptied the three saddlebags. He counted thirty mint shipping pouches. Each carried one hundred gold double eagles. Sixty thousand dollars, five pouches to a man.

Nixon hefted his saddlebag. "Hell of a night's work."

Bass spat. "Yah, well ride smart and you might get to enjoy it."

"Ride smart meaning?"

"Meaning we ride north to the Platte. We split up there and use the river to cover our tracks."

They mounted up. Bass led them north through the night. They reached the banks of the North Platte as the sky turned a predawn gray. They paused to water the horses.

"You boys head west. Split up when you see the chance."

Collins cocked an eye. "Where you goin' Sam?"

"None of us need to know the answer to that question for any of us."

"But I just figured, since we been ridin' together."

"You figured wrong, Joel. We split here. You go on with the rest. Now get out of here."

Nixon and the others splashed into the stream along the riverbank. Collins stared at Bass for a moment in disbelief. He saw no give in the set of Bass's jaw. He wheeled his horse into the stream and followed the others.

Bass watched them go, confident he'd get home. He waited until the others were well out of sight and sound before turning his horse downstream, doubling back on their trail.

Shady Grove
The colonel paused to yawn. His chin nodded to his chest. A light footstep sounded up the porch. She appeared as if on cue.

I pretended to review my notes, watching her approach. Her eyes smiled. I'm not sure I fooled her.

"Time for lunch, Colonel."

She had a velvety voice flavored in butterscotch.

He bobbed awake. One eye peeked under a bushy brow. He glanced from his attendant apparition to me.

"Penny isn't it?"

She blushed ever so lightly. "It 'tis."

I marked a hint of Irish brogue.

"The scribe here is Robert Brentwood. His facility with the written word must exceed his capacity for the spoken word. I presume to introduce you to him for the simple fact a man my age may not live long enough to see him do it for himself."

We blushed. Crook winked, pleased with himself.

"Mr. Brentwood, Penny O'Malley. I've drawn the short straw to give care to this old rascal."

"Please accept my condolences."

She laughed a merry throaty laugh. Crook scowled at the turn of the table.

"And please, call me Robert."

"Very well then, Robert, you must call me Penny."

The colonel straightened in his chair. "I see my work here is very nearly done. Now if you will invite this young lady to tea, I shall be content to go to the drivel they call lunch."

I favored the old man with a conspiratorial smile. "She strikes me as more an ice cream sundae sort of lass."

She laughed again. "Don't tell me you're Irish, Robert Brent-wood."

I shook my head with a smile. "Only a wee dram on me sainted mother's side."

"Where the Irish are concerned sir, there's no such thing as a wee dram. And yes, I do like an ice cream sundae."

"Splendid," Crook said. "You do owe me boy."

I watched her wheel him away. Ice cream on Sunday seemed a long day to wait.

Six

Shady Grove

The following Saturday arrived on a swirl of early winter snow. I was shown to a cozy lounge for my interview with Colonel Crook. Penny rolled him down a long hall with a waxed wooden floor leading to the visitor's lounge. She looked fetching as ever, though I had to admit she looked positively stunning in the simple floral dress she'd worn to the ice cream parlor the previous Sunday. Her eyes brightened that Mona Lisa smile as she rolled the colonel to a stop across from my chair. I stood.

"Robert."

"Penny. Is he behaving himself today?"

"He's been incorrigible with questions all week."

"I'm not surprised."

"Good afternoon to you too, Robert."

I recovered. "Good afternoon, Colonel."

"Now about that book of yours, or have you taken up another interest?"

"I have." She blushed. I liked it. "But I do believe we should continue with the book as well."

"For lack of a respectable excuse to continue these flirtations of yours?"

Buffalo Station
September 19, 5:30 a.m.
What the hell is going on? The damn train is three hours late and not

a peep out of Big Springs! Ben Wise snapped his watchcase closed. It smelled like trouble. He paced the station, turning the situation over in his mind. She left Cheyenne on schedule. For whatever reason he couldn't get a telegraph acknowledgment out of Big Springs. Indians cut the lines quite often in the early days, though that hadn't been much of a problem in recent years. He got through to Cheyenne, so the trouble had to be at Big Springs. Was it the telegraph connection or something worse? Wise had a bad feeling he couldn't explain.

The familiar whistle blasts—a short, then a long—sounded in the distance. *Finally!* He let loose his pent-up tensions. Still there'd be hell to pay for the schedule. He threw on his hat and coat and stepped out onto the platform. The rain had cleared through. A fresh breeze mingled the scents of rain and sage. Off to the west the headlamp appeared around the mile marker bend. Wise headed toward the watering station. He'd have the tank ready the minute she stopped.

The engine ground to a stop, screaming steel and belching gouts of steam. Wise caught the chain ready to swing the watering trough into place. The engineer waved from the cab. "I'll take care of that Ben. You best see to your telegraph key. The Pinkerton will want to wire Cheyenne. We've been robbed!"

North Platte

Nixon called a halt to rest the horses on the grassy riverbank as the sun climbed toward midday. Sunlight glittered on the eastward course of the river. Not far upstream a rocky wash spilled out of the hillside to the river. He nudged Berry and pointed with his chin. "Looks like a good spot to turn north. Collins and Heffridge can go on and find their own way out."

Berry nodded. "We'll make better time than ploddin' along at the river's edge."

Nixon walked over to where Collins rested against a tree

trunk. "Joel, me and Jim will be leavin' you at that wash up yonder. You and Bill can stick to the river a bit further and pick your way out."

Collins wouldn't have chosen Heffridge for a partner, but when Bass went off on his own he guessed that's how things would wind up. Bass kind of soured on him after the poker game in Deadwood so he wasn't surprised when the partnership ended. Sam took the lead of the outfit when Nixon and his boys joined up. Nixon pretty well had things his way before that. When Bass left, Nixon took up where he left things. He and Berry were tight. That left him with Heffridge. With his share of the gold, he wouldn't need the man very long.

Julesburg
September 19

A dark, ragged line of rooftops broke the green gold sea of prairie grass lapping at the shore of a bright blue southern sky. Heffridge glanced nervously over his shoulder at their back trail. "You really think this is a good idea Collins?"

"Last place they'd look for us, besides we need supplies to make it to Dodge." The idea of following the rail bed southeast from Julesburg struck him as a great plan. They could cover a lot of ground fast and leave very little trail for pursuit to follow if anyone did figure it out.

"How long you figure on stayin' here?"

"No more than tonight and enough of tomorrow to get provisioned."

They rode into the east end of town, south of the tracks. The livery amounted to a corral and a blacksmith's shop with a loft. Collins drew rein. "You stay with the horses, Heff. I'll take care of this."

Dim light filtered through a dusty window and the occasional chink in the plank shed. He found the proprietor smith at his forge, pumping the bellows.

"What can I do for you?" His deep voice rumbled from a barrel chest. The buttons and sleeves of a dirty red union suit strained against his muscled bulk. He wore a heavy leather apron over wool britches held up by sweat-stained suspenders.

"Got a couple of horses to put up for the night."

"Fifty cents each."

Collins fished a silver dollar out of his pocket and tossed it to the smith. He caught it, turned it over in dark stained fingers and stuffed it in his pocket.

"Put 'em in the corral. They'll be waitin' in the mornin'."

"You wouldn't happen to know of a packhorse that might be for sale?"

The smith arched an eyebrow and cracked what passed for a smile. "Not a horse, but I got a saddle-broke jenny I might let you have."

"I ain't never had much luck with mules."

"Oh this one's real sweet. She'll do you good. You put up your horses. I'll bring her in so you can have a look at her."

By the time they unsaddled the horses and turned them out, the smith had a sturdy, brown-eyed buckskin mule cross tied in the shop doorway. Heffridge checked her hooves and hocks. He threw a packsaddle up on her back. She stood quietly. He took her halter lead and led her around the stable yard. She moved willingly with no sign of sass or temper. He led her back to the cross tie and gave Collins his opinion. "Good mule."

"How much?"

"She's four-year-old prime. Fifty dollars seems more than fair."

"More than fair is right. It's a damn mule. I'll give you forty dollars if you throw in the packsaddle and not a penny more."

The smith scratched the dark stubble of beard at his chin. "I'm bein' cheated here, but it's late. You got yourself a mule."

Collins tossed him two coins. The bright gold double eagles caught the lantern light. The smith caught them in a soot-stained fist and held one up to the light.

"We'll pick her up in the morning with the horses. Now where might a feller find a room for the night?"

The big man scowled. "South Platte's the only hotel in town if that's what you mean. Otherwise Sadie and one of her girls over at the Rusty Spike might put you up if you was to stand for the price."

A whore for the night? Collins could afford that. So could the dull-witted Heffridge. "Much obliged."

Sadie eyed the two strangers. The Rusty Spike had a few regulars. Newcomers stood out. Things weren't at all like the end-of-track heydays anymore. Chipped paint and scarred surroundings testified to that. The only surface in the place that had a shine was the bar top, owing to the bartender's boredom. The shorter one had the cocksure attitude of a bandy rooster. He looked like trouble. The big one had a bovine look like he might have an ox somewhere in his breeding. She shuddered. The shorter one smiled at her. She smiled back. It was her job. He came over like a fish on a line.

"Where can I find Sadie?"

"You found her."

"Joel Collins is the name. The feller over at the livery said you might put a man up for the night."

She knew the type. Held a higher opinion of himself than he could ever back up. Still booked for the night was booked for the night. She lifted her chin to the oxy one. "What about him?"

"Him too."

She glanced at a plump blonde with laudanum-vacant eyes, leaning against the bar. "What say Tilley?"

She giggled.

"That'll be twenty dollars each, startin' with drinks."

The short one tossed her a mint-new double eagle. She made a show of tucking it in the opulent swell overflowing the bodice of her dress. "Come on, Joel Collins, you done married yourself a wife for the night."

She led the way to a corner table and motioned the bartender for a bottle and glasses. *Get him drunk enough she might even get a good night's sleep in the bargain.*

SEVEN

September 20

Dusty light filtered through window grime bathed the Rusty Spike in a sepia morning glow. Sadie sat at a corner table nursing a cup of coffee and a bad head. The little shit could drink and keep it up. So much for a good night's sleep. She pushed at an errant strand of auburn hair. She turned the gold double eagle in a small circle on the scarred tabletop with a chipped fingernail.

The town buzzed with news of the Big Springs robbery. Sixty thousand dollars was a king's ransom. She'd heard the talk. The Union Pacific was offering a thousand-dollar reward for information leading to the capture of those responsible. A thousand dollars could get a girl's attention. Having a mint-new gold double eagle didn't make a man a train robber. Heaven knew the Rusty Spike saw enough double eagles, but something about that pair didn't sit right. They didn't have the appearance of businessmen or wealthy travelers. They were rough-cut and well armed. They just happened to have money, maybe a lot of money. The reward offer said to report any information to the nearest Pinkerton agency. That'd be the one up at the depot.

Tall, muscular and handsome, Beauregard Longstreet's family roots ran deep in the old South. He came from the fringes of the more prominent Longstreet line best known for his cousin, the distinguished general who served under Robert E. Lee.

Beau had never been West Point material. He parlayed his family name into a junior officer's appointment and rose to the rank of captain before the cessation of hostilities. Humiliated in defeat, he drifted west, reaching Saint Louis penniless. He signed on as a Pinkerton guard out of necessity. He soon demonstrated a knack for protection. They'd done a good deal of defending in the later stages of the war. His experience as a field commander distinguished his performance. He gained greater responsibility in his assignments as the company followed the railroads and goldfields west.

Pinkerton put him on the next train to Julesburg as part of the team investigating the Big Springs robbery. He figured the next stop up the line from the scene might be close enough to be interesting. That was before he got to Julesburg. He set up shop at the depot and put out the company offer of a reward for information leading to the apprehension of those responsible. Since then there'd been nothing to do but wait. The wait he concluded was for orders to get out of this shit hole. No self-respecting train robber with sixty thousand dollars in gold would be found dead in a dump like this.

He rocked the barrel-backed chair away from the small desk the stationmaster had given him in the corner of the passenger lounge and loosened his starched collar in the crook of an index finger. He stifled a yawn as he gazed out the dust-streaked window across a rolling sea of prairie grass stretching north and west to the skyline. The soft scrape of a light footstep on the plank floor at his back called him back to his present.

He twisted around his chair's groan. The woman wore a black lace shawl over a low-cut lavender gown in a failed attempt at modesty. Her red hair piled high in disheveled wispy ringlets. Watery green eyes lent an air of vulnerability to a face that remained somehow soft and pretty, despite the hard edges imposed by the harsh life of a frontier working girl.

"Good afternoon ma'am, Beau Longstreet at your service."

"Sadie, Sadie Sawyer," she mumbled.

"Pleased to meet you, Miss Sawyer. How may I be of service?"

Handsome devil with a syrupy Southern drawl, nice. "Please, call me Sadie. It's about the reward."

"You have information about the Big Springs robbery?"

She nodded fumbling with the drawstrings to a faded blue purse. "I may. I have a suspicion." She handed him a bright new twenty-dollar gold piece.

"There's no law against havin' a new gold piece. Then again, you don't see many as new as this. Where'd you get it?"

"Ah, a customer give it to me. Me and Tilley entertained a couple of gents at the Rusty Spike. One calls himself Collins, the other says his name is Heffridge."

"What makes them suspicious?"

"The one calls himself Heffridge let his whiskey talk a little loose. He told Tilley, 'There's lots more where that one came from.' What would you think?"

"Yes, I see your point. Where are these two now?"

She shrugged.

"When did they hit town?"

"Yesterday I reckon. They showed up at the Rusty Spike lookin' for a place to stay the night."

"Did they?"

She shifted one hand to her hip suggestively and pointed to the double eagle with her chin. "And where do you suppose that came from handsome?"

"Yes, of course. Where are they now?"

She shrugged. "They left early this morning."

"Any idea where they went?"

She shook her head. "I listen. I ain't paid to talk much."

Longstreet suppressed a smile. "What do they look like?"

"Collins is on the small side. Got a chip on his shoulder that one. I expect he's trouble. Heffridge is a big dumb ox. I doubt he'd know enough to come in out of the rain."

"With a description like that, finding them should be no trouble at all. Are you sure there isn't anything more you can tell me?"

She pursed her full lips. "Yeah, they must have stabled their horses at the livery. Collins said the blacksmith sent them our way."

He made a note.

She smiled. "Now put me down for that reward and come by anytime to pay a girl a call. I'd make you right welcome." She turned on a flounce of petticoat ruffles and headed for the door with a come-hither sway to her hips.

Beau chuckled to himself. *Right welcome and a gait to go with it.*

Shady Grove

Gray shadow crept across the polished tile floor of the visitor's lounge. The colonel paused. He knit his brows.

"I think that's about enough for today, Robert. Penny will be along directly to fetch me to supper. Will you be coming tomorrow?"

I shook my head. "I'm afraid I have another engagement."

"Engagement is it? I hadn't expected a man of your deliberate caution would move so swiftly."

"Sir?"

"Tomorrow is Sunday. I should have thought you more likely to advance your cause with another sundae. Butterscotch I believe is the preferred flavor."

"If you must know, Colonel, we plan to take in a new motion-picture show."

"Oh. Quite an adventurous choice. My advice is follow it up with ice cream. You can't go wrong with ice cream."

"Thank you, sir. I appreciate your . . . thoughtfulness."

He smiled. "Now about my gratuity."

"Gratuity?"

"Yes, a small token of appreciation you can do me for kindling this new romance in your life. You may think of it as an advance on my part in the royalties for this book I'm helping you write."

"Did you have something specific in mind?"

"I do." He glanced up the hallway with a conspiratorial twinkle in his eye.

"Whiskey."

"Whiskey?"

"Yes whiskey. They don't let a man have a drop in this place. Can you imagine? It borders on barbaric. If you'd be kind enough to . . ."

He broke off his request at the clip of heel on tile. The look in his eye spoke the rest with a warning.

I half smiled and nodded. My back to the sound I sensed the sweet scent of vanilla. I stood and smiled. Her eyes smiled back.

"Time for supper, Colonel."

"Time for supper, hell it's time for a drink."

"Now Colonel, you know the rules. Let's not start that again." She started to turn his chair to the hall.

"Can you imagine, Robert? An Irish girl with so little sympathy for a man's thirst, it's unnatural."

He shot me a helpless glance. I winked, the bargain sealed.

"Yes, well enjoy the picture show, both of you. See you next week, Robert."

She gave me a 'Did you really have to tell him' look over her shoulder as she wheeled him away. I shrugged.

The motion-picture show was a Western with a lovely heroine in distress and a handsome cowboy hero, riding a beautiful sorrel horse that might have been the smartest actor in the film. The sorrel seems to fill that role in picture shows, its distinctive markings set off to best advantage in black and white. We shared a sundae after the show. I walked her home in the gathering darkness of early evening. It must have been the darkness there on the porch, rather black and white like the picture show when I kissed her. She still tasted of butterscotch.

It snowed all Friday night. By the time I made my purchase and trudged through the snow to Shady Grove, I arrived an hour later than my usual time. The attendant in reception showed me to the visitor's parlor. I waited. She rolled him into the parlor.

"You're late, Robert."

"I'm sorry, sir. The snow, I hope you understand."

"Me understand? My dear boy, it's this past hour's anguish for this poor enfeebled young woman you've completely flummoxed for the past week."

"Colonel! You hush now." She blushed.

I laughed. "I have no idea what you are talking about."

"There may be no fool like an old fool, but you can't fool one either."

She laughed. "I can tell when I'm no longer needed. I shall leave you two to your nefarious purposes."

She treated me to her Mona Lisa and heavenly stride.

The colonel watched until he was satisfied she was out of hearing. "Have you got it?"

"Got what?"

"Our bargain. You agreed. Don't tell me a young buck like you is forgetful."

I took my seat. I fumbled in my coat for my pencil and pad pretending to ignore the question. "You know you really shouldn't embarrass her so."

"It is one of the few pleasures left to an old fart like me when you're confined to a place like this. Now did you bring me a bottle?"

I reached inside my coat. "You know this is against my better judgment."

"What better judgment? You're a pup. And a lovesick pup I'll wager thanks to my better judgment." He held out his hand.

I passed him the bottle. He sequestered it beneath his blanket. "Not a word now."

I shook my head. "And implicate my own complicity? I should think not. Now shall we begin?"

"Where were we?"

"The whore alerted the Pinkerton man."

"Ah yes . . ."

EIGHT

Julesburg
September 22

Cane rode into Julesburg two days after the robbery report reached Sydney. He decided to stay the night and move on to Big Springs in the morning. He jogged into the windswept west end of town followed by a lazy sage ball. *South Platte Hotel,* the cracked signboard read. Not much to look at for sure. Still it looked like a roof over a man's head with a hot meal and a drink somewhere nearby. He stepped down at a hitch rack recently repaired, judging by the green wood. He looped a rein over the rail, threw his saddlebags over his shoulder and stepped up the boardwalk fronting the hotel. He entered a small shadow-cast lobby with a deserted registration desk. No need to light a lamp he guessed, unless somebody needed to see. He rang the bell on the counter and waited. A stair creaked in the gloom off to the left. Boots clumped down a narrow stairway accompanied by the rattle of a scrub mop and bucket. Now there's an encouraging sign.

A dark hulk reached the bottom of the stairs. "Sorry, I ain't lit the lamp down here yet."

Cane chuckled. "I noticed."

A lucifer flared behind the counter. The rawboned clerk wearing shirtsleeves and an apron lifted a soot-smudged chimney and lit the lamp. He blew out the match and trimmed the wick. "That's better. Now what can I do for you?"

"I need a room for the night."

The clerk spun the register. "That'll be two dollars."

Cane slid the coins across the counter with a scowl. "Kind of pricey."

"You pay for the best in town."

"I didn't see another hotel in town."

"That's right, you didn't. That makes us the best in town." The clerk passed a key across the counter. "Room two, top of the stairs, fresh scrubbed to boot, no extra charge."

"Much obliged. I need a place to stable my horse."

"Livery and blacksmith's down the street." He hooked a thumb east. "Best eating in town is my brother's place next door."

"Your brother's place, I see. How about a drink?"

"Rusty Spike." He tossed his head. "Yonder across the street."

Cane hefted his saddlebags and climbed the creaky stairs to room two. He found the small room better lit than the lobby, courtesy of a dirty, lace-curtained window, catching the last fast-fading daylight. He dropped his saddlebags on the small bed. A wooden dresser, table and oil lamp completed the furnishings. He cracked the window open in hopes of catching a fresh evening breeze.

Back outside he led Smoke down the street to the blacksmith shop and livery. He found a stocky barrel-chested smith folding his heavy leather apron preparing to close for the night.

"Got room for one more?"

The man sized up the late arrival. "How long he gonna be here?"

"Just overnight."

"That'll be fifty cents. You can put your tack in the shed. I'll take care of water, a scoop and some hay."

"Much obliged." Cane fished a dollar out of his pants pocket and handed it over.

The smith drew a handful of coins from his pocket searching for change. A bright gold double eagle caught the dim light.

"That one looks like it might still be warm from the mint."

The smith arched an eyebrow. "It's new."

"How'd you come by it?"

"What's it to you?"

"The Union Pacific lost a passel of 'em three days ago."

"So I hear. No law against holdin' a double eagle. You the law?"

"Bounty hunter."

"Pinkerton, bounty hunter. Seems these boys is real popular with everybody but real lawmen."

"Pinkerton?"

"Yeah. Fella named Longstreet come by yesterday askin' after the same pair."

"What did you tell him?"

"Ask him. I ain't in the bounty business."

Cane fished a five-dollar gold piece out of his pocket. "This help your memory any?"

The smith eyed the coin. "Picked up their horses and rode out early day before yesterday. Rode southeast on takin' their leave." He held out his hand.

Cane held the coin. "How'd you come by that double eagle?"

"Sold a pack mule to 'em when they rode in."

"Any idea what they did while they was in town?"

"Went up to the Rusty Spike is all I know."

"Sounds like a popular spot."

"Depends on what you're lookin' for. Ask for Sadie. She might know what become of them."

"Much obliged."

Cane surveyed the scene from the bat wings. The atmosphere in the Rusty Spike suited its name. Unlike the raucous clamor of a boomtown saloon like the Last Stop, the Spike settled for the faded glory left over from more vibrant times. A quiet card game or two and a few hard-rode soiled doves served the needs of those inclined to a local watering hole. He stepped up to the bar and signaled the bartender, a balding man with flabby jowls, waxed mustache and large belly covered in a stained apron. He sauntered down the bar wiping a glass with a towel in desperate need of a washtub.

"What'll it be stranger?"

"Whiskey."

The bartender set the glass on the bar. He pulled a bottle off the back bar and poured. He set the bottle on the bar and started to walk away.

"Where can I find Sadie?"

The bartender paused and jerked a thumb toward three doves lounging at a back corner table.

"How about another glass?" The bartender set one on the bar and moved off. Cane turned the glass over the neck of the bottle, picked it up and headed back to Sadie's table.

"Sadie?" The redhead looked up, a flicker of interest in her eye. "Care for a drink?"

"Excuse me ladies." She rose, the hint of a smile playing at the corners of her full red lips.

Cane led the way to a nearby table and held back a chair. She brushed his hand taking her seat.

"To what do I owe the pleasure, Mr. . . . ?" Her voice trailed off.

"Cane, Briscoe Cane." He poured.

"Like I said, Briscoe Cane, to what do I owe the pleasure?"

"I'm lookin' for a couple of men. Someone thought you might have seen them."

"Pity."

"How's that?"

"I thought you might have been sent by a satisfied customer, if you know what I mean."

"I'm sure that happens quite regular."

"Not like the looks of you." She took a long pull on her drink and held out the glass. "Who might these two be?"

Cane poured. "Sam Bass, travels with a man name of Collins."

Sadie eyed him over the rim of her glass with naked interest. "Don't know anyone named Bass. Collins come through a couple days ago with a feller called Heffridge."

Cane scowled. "Short guy with a mustache and an attitude?"

"That's him."

What the hell happened to Bass? Clearly they'd split up. The realization dawned. Bass might have gotten away.

"You think he's mixed up in that Big Springs train robbery don't you?"

Cane snapped back from the prospect of frustration. "I didn't say that. What makes you bring it up?"

"Cause I think he was and so do the Pinkertons."

"What makes you say that?"

"Them two threw around brand-new gold double eagles and bragged there was more where they came from. I give my information to the Pinkerton man up to the depot. They're offerin' a reward you know."

"I didn't know that." The whore's eyes strayed over his shoulder toward the door with a flicker of recognition. He heard boots clip the plank floor coming toward them. He eased back from the table, making room for his gun and kicking himself for leaving his back to the door. He knew better than that.

"Evenin' Miss Sadie."

Cane glanced over his shoulder. The big man with dark eyes and a barbered mustache wore a bowler hat and frock coat with a bulge under the left arm.

"Forgive the intrusion. I've a few more questions to ask."

"Might as well sit down and join us Mr. Longstreet. Briscoe Cane here and me was just discussin' Collins and Heffridge."

Longstreet cut his eyes to Cane. "Beau Longstreet, Pinkerton agent." He stuck out his hand.

"Briscoe Cane, bounty hunter."

Longstreet pulled up a chair. Sadie signaled the bartender for another glass.

"So Mr. Cane what's your interest in the Big Springs robbery?"

"I been on the trail of Bass and Collins long before Big Springs. Call me Briscoe."

"My pleasure, my friends call me Beau. Your mention of Bass is interesting. Our agents on the scene at Big Springs also think he was involved. The gang divided the loot and split up not far out of town. They used the river to cover their tracks."

"It ain't quite trail sign, but if they keep droppin' them new double eagles we sure as hell ought to be able to find 'em."

"I quite agree."

Sadie gave Longstreet a playful pinch on the cheek to remind him he'd come to see her. "You two big handsome boys just go round up them crooks right quick and bring me my reward."

Longstreet smiled.

The bat wings flew open to the clump of boots and the ring of spurs. Three hard cases trooped in.

Sadie went round eyed over Cane's shoulder with a small gasp.

Shit bein' in the wrong chair was becomin' a habit in the presence of this woman. Cane eased his chair away from the table angled toward the bar where he could see the door. Three well armed young toughs filled the entrance. The leader, a hawk-featured gun hand dressed in black had fire in his eye and a thin scar splitting the corner of his lower lip. He swept the room with his eyes clearly looking for something or someone.

"Sadie darlin' I got a need fit to drive a fence post!"

The Rusty Spike fell silent. Sadie shrank back as though trying to disappear into the back of her chair. Longstreet cut his eyes to Cane and then to Sadie. "Who's that?" he hissed.

"Braylin Cross," she whispered, her voice barely audible.

Cane had heard of him. Mean as a scorpion and said to be near as fast.

"Well now, seems like you got a couple of friends callin'. You boys won't mind runnin' along so me and Sadie here can have us a romantic reunion. Hear that boys?" He called over his shoulder. "It's a reunion. I kinda like that."

The two toughs laughed. Sadie winced.

Longstreet rose from his chair, drawing himself up to his full height. Cane slipped out of his chair and backed away from the table. Cross brushed past Longstreet toward Sadie. Longstreet barred his way with an arm.

"I beg your pardon, sir. I don't believe the lady desires the pleasure of your company this evening."

Cross paused. He looked down at Longstreet's arm in stunned disbelief. "You ready to die for a whore, Johnny Reb?"

"I'm sure that won't be necessary. You're simply going to take your 'fence post drivin' need' and your friends over there and leave."

Cross laughed over his shoulder. "You hear that boys? Sadie's gentleman friend here thinks he's gonna throw us out of here."

Cross made a move to draw. Longstreet dropped the fist of his restraining arm hard on the gunman's forearm. The tough's gun hand went limp, the pistol fell harmlessly to the floor. In an instant Longstreet's nickel-plated .38 pocket pistol flashed from its shoulder holster to a cocked position beside Cross's eyes.

The room exploded in muzzle flashes, powder charge and smoke as Cross's men made their plays. Cane hit the first one twice before he cleared leather. Longstreet shot the second over

Cross's shoulder, returning the pistol to the gunny's temple while Cane finished the second man. The Rusty Spike fell silent.

Longstreet grasped Cross by the shirt collar and returned his pistol to its shoulder holster. He doubled Cross over in a rush of breath with a gut punch to rival a mule kick. A vicious uppercut snapped the gunny's head back. Longstreet squared off with a left-right-cross combination that sent gouts of blood flying from his shattered nose and mouth. Cross sprawled on his back, disarmed and beaten. Longstreet yanked the gunfighter to his feet by his shirt collar and gun belt. He propelled the man to the bat wings and threw him into the street. "Now get your sorry ass on your horse and get out of town before I lose my temper."

Longstreet strode back into the saloon and crossed the room to the table. He nodded his appreciation to Cane. "Nice shooting." He took his seat. "I do believe I'll have that drink now." Sadie poured, her hand trembling noticeably. "I apologize for that unfortunate display Miss Sadie. I hope you will forgive me."

She dropped her hands to her lap and lowered her eyes. She took a deep breath, steadying herself. Longstreet filled her glass. She glanced up, favoring him with a small smile. "Forgive you?" She shook her head. "No. Thank you. He's . . ." Her voice trailed off. "He's a vicious man, that one. He likes to hurt women. Last time he was here I thought he might kill me."

"I don't expect he'll be back anytime soon."

Her eyes lifted to his. The fear drained way, softened at the sight of him.

Cane decided he'd become about as useful here as a third handle on a plow.

Longstreet continued gently. "If you are up to it, I still have a few questions I'd like to ask you."

NINE

September 23

Cane mulled the problem, saddling Smoke the following morning. He didn't have much to go on. The smith said they rode out following the rail bed. Heat waves shimmered along the rails, disappearing in the distance to the southeast. That wouldn't leave much of a trail. It also doubled back through Big Springs which struck Cane as bold and smart. The law would be long past looking for them at the scene of the holdup. One thing he did know, the Big Springs holdup raised the stakes for the pair he was after. Pinkerton was offering a thousand-dollar reward for information. No telling what their contract with Union Pacific was worth. It seemed like a fine time to see just how much this Colonel Crook and his Great Western Detective League might really be worth.

Finished with his cinch he dropped the stirrup fender and stepped into the saddle. He squeezed up a jog up the road to the depot. As he stepped down, Longstreet came out to the platform.

"Mornin' Briscoe."

"Mornin' Beau." He ground tied Smoke and clumped the platform step.

"I telegraphed our agents as far east as Dodge to be on the lookout for Collins and Heffridge. I haven't received word that anyone's seen them."

"Probably a little soon for that. They got a telegrapher in there?"

"Sure do. Need to send a wire?"

"Yup."

He left the Pinkerton to wonder what that might be about. Dusty brown light filtered through the depot windows, spilling in rusty puddles across the stained plank floor. Lean and lanky the telegrapher glanced up from his key peering at Cane through a green eyeshade.

"What can I do for you stranger?"

"I need to send a wire."

"Paper and pencil is on the counter."

Longstreet lounged against the depot wall when Cane returned to the platform.

"Get your wire sent?"

"I did."

"Now what?"

Cane tossed his head southeasterly. "Lacking the reach of the Eye that Never Sleeps, I reckon followin' Collins and Heffridge is the best lead I got."

Longstreet chuckled at Cane's mocking reference to Pinkerton's well-known motto.

"If they stick to the line, they'll skirt Big Springs. They're well supplied according to the clerk at the general store. I expect I'll catch up with them."

"I hope you do. Collins might be the best way to get a line on Bass."

Cane nodded. "You did a nice job on Cross last night. Did you know who you was up against?"

"Not really. I found out later."

"That's one dangerous son of a bitch. You whipped him and sent him packin' but I'd watch my back if I was you."

"Thanks for the advice. The other two would have gotten me if it hadn't been for you. I'm much obliged."

"No trouble, though the next time you go takin' on the likes of a Braylin Cross, it might be best to know you had competent backup before the shooting starts."

Longstreet laughed. "Never doubted it for a minute. Thanks again for the advice though."

"All's well that ends well, I guess. And besides, you got yourself one grateful whore there."

"Not my style."

"I didn't say she was your style. I just said she was grateful. There's a difference that just might be fun."

"Too bad you're not stickin' around Cane. I think we might make a good team."

"I generally work alone, but maybe someday, Beau. If you take my advice and don't get yourself killed that is." He gathered Smoke's reins and stepped up. He touched the brim of his hat. "Get up there." He squeezed up a lope with a wave.

Shady Grove

It was my turn to stretch. I had writer's cramp. Fading light seeping through the parlor windows foretold the end to another session. As if on cue Penny appeared.

"Time for supper, Colonel. I'll see you later, Robert."

"Later? What romantic rendezvous have you planned for a Saturday night?"

"If you must know, Penny is accompanying me to a dance at the Grange Hall this evening."

"A dance. Lost our taste for ice cream have we?"

"That's for Sunday."

"Robert, you've only to turn her head on the weekend. I on the other hand must deal with the aftereffects of all this courting the whole of the next week. I'm beginning to question my own better judgment in setting this whole affair in motion."

"We all have our lapses in judgment don't we, Colonel." I eyed his lap.

A smile puffed his mustache and creased the corners of his eyes. He patted his lap robe. "Yes we do. Until next week then Robert."

The following Saturday I arrived at Shady Grove Rest Home and Convalescent Center at my usual hour with a bottle of fine Kentucky bourbon bundled in my coat. Penny and I enjoyed the previous weekend, growing evermore comfortable in our time spent together. Between that and my excitement over our progress with the book, I found myself looking forward to these sessions with the irascible Colonel Crook. She wheeled him down the hall to the visitor's parlor. Our eyes met. The colonel coughed.

"Good afternoon, Robert."

"Good afternoon, Colonel. You're looking well."

"Humpf. Better than my circumstances if you must know."

I favored Penny with a wink. "Has he been behaving himself this week?"

"After a fashion." She dispensed a Mona Lisa. "He's yours until supper. I'll be back to claim him then."

I watched her depart.

"We can begin whenever you've had your fill."

"I believe you instigated this romance." I took my seat.

"You were the one drooling like a moon-eyed pup."

"Well, congratulations. Things seem to be working out quite nicely." I drew my notebook and pencil from a coat pocket.

"Before we begin, have you anything else in there for me?"

I smiled and glanced over his shoulder conspiratorially before handing him the bottle. He tucked it under his blanket and handed me last week's empty.

"What's this?"

"What does it look like?"

"So I'm also to take out the trash as part of this grand bargain."

"How else would you have me dispose of the contraband?"

"I should think a man of your vast criminal experience would have no trouble at all dealing with so trivial a problem."

"As you can plainly see, I have no problem dealing with it. I have you. Now where were we?"

I consulted my notes. "Cane sent a wire from Julesburg and bid his good-bye to Longstreet."

"Ah, yes." His eyes twinkled. "That's when I began to appreciate how well suited Mr. Cane was to the work of the Great Western Detective League. The wire was sent to our Denver offices. The Western Union messenger delivered it to me personally. Cane reported that the perpetrators responsible for the Wells Fargo holdup were one Sam Bass and his partner Joel Collins. They had, he informed me, subsequently joined forces with a hitherto-unknown band of miscreants named Nixon, Berry and Heffridge. But then he came to the truly important part of his report. Bass, Collins and their newfound friends were none other than those responsible for the Big Springs train robbery. He noted that the Union Pacific had the Pinkerton agency engaged in investigating the case, though having ascertained the information available to the local agent on the scene, he believed himself to be in the better position to apprehend the thieves. He then reasoned, rightly as it turned out, that the railroad might offer a suitable addition to our reward for the recovery of its stolen shipment. Forthwith I instructed him by return wire to continue his pursuit of the perpetrators whilst I sought Union Pacific recompense for the capture of those responsible and the recovery, if possible, of the stolen gold."

"So Cane saw the prospect for something of a competition between the Great Western Detective League and Pinkerton?"

"Precisely, and as subsequent events would unfold, this was the first of many cases where justice was served by the rivalry between agencies contending for notoriety and reward."

Big Springs

Collins drew a halt. The silvery ribbon of track stretched to the east, growing narrow before it disappeared in the heat.

"Close enough."

Heffridge spit a stream of tobacco juice into the dust at his horse's hock. "Close enough to what?"

"Close enough to Big Springs. We're turnin' south."

"I thought we was headed for Kansas."

"We are. In case you forgot, somebody robbed a train up yonder a few days ago. I expect the UP ain't forgot. The place will be crawlin' with Pinkerton men. It ain't big enough to hide a horsefly. We'd get noticed for sure. We're gonna give Big Springs a wide berth. We'll circle east some. We can head back north when we're clear. Maybe catch an eastbound train at Buffalo Station. We'll travel faster that way and in some improved comfort."

"We're gonna ride the train?"

"Yup. Last place they'd look for us I reckon."

"How far east you figurin' to go?"

"Dodge, maybe Kansas City. They got some fine women in Kansas City."

"Speakin' of women, how 'bout takin' this lead rope for a spell. You talk about ridin' in comfort. Hell, I'd settle for not draggin' this pack mule."

"I ain't partial to mules."

"So you said. Then again fair's fair." He held out the halter lead. "Come on now, she's real sweet. You'll see."

He shook his head and took the rope. He dallied it to his saddle horn and wheeled south.

Buffalo Station

Bass crested a rise northwest of town. The commercial center of Buffalo Station sprawled along the tracks north of the depot that gave it its name. Stores and saloons were visible along with a livery and a hotel. Fancy that. Clean sheets and maybe something soft and tart to slip between them. He was about ready for a break from his travels. Texas could wait a few days while he enjoyed some of the gold burning a hole in his pocket. He eased the roan down the slope toward the west end of town.

A sage ball tumbled down the street ahead of his passage. He took in the town up one side of the street and down the other. He composed a list as the possibilities presented themselves. He registered a shave, a bath, a room, a hot meal and a saloon to prowl. Whiskey, women and cards, the saloon beckoned. He wheeled his horse to the hotel hitch rack and stepped down. He tied off a rein and hoisted his heavily loaded saddlebags over his shoulder. He clumped up the boardwalk to the dimly lit lobby. He crossed the neatly appointed room with a polished floor to the deserted counter. He tapped the bell for service. An attractive woman appeared from a small office off the end of the counter.

"May I help you?"

She had a rose petal complexion, green eyes and auburn hair piled in a soft swell of curl. She wore a modest gray gown that turned out an ample bodice to breathtaking effect. He must have stared. He forgot to speak.

"May I help you?" She smiled, showing even white teeth.

"I, ah, I need a room."

"That we have." She spun the register. "Sign here, Mr. . . ."

"Bass, Sam Bass." He took the pen from the ink pot and signed.

"That will be a dollar a night, Mr. Bass. Will you be staying long?"

"I don't know for certain."

She held his eyes with that smile again. "Well let's hope you stay long enough to take advantage of everything Buffalo Station has to offer."

"Perhaps I should make a point of that, Mrs. . . . ."

"Stone, Abigail Stone, my friends call me Abby." She offered her hand. "And it's Miss, Mr. Bass."

He accepted. "Please, call me Sam."

"Then you must call me Abby."

"Fair enough. Now for a start on the things Buffalo Station has to offer I need a barber, a bath and a hot meal."

She tilted her chin with an arch in her brow as though amused by the request. "A bath and a barber, I'm impressed. Buffalo Station can take care of all of those things. The barbershop is two doors down the street. Silas, that's the barber, maintains a bathhouse in his backroom. For a hot meal, I recommend Delmonico's across the street."

"Would you care to join me? You could fill me in on the rest of the things Buffalo Station has to offer."

Her eyes turned smoky with a half smile. "My night man comes on at six o'clock."

"Shall I meet you here then?"

"You may." She slid a key across the counter. "Room four, top of the stairs."

TEN

Julesburg

Boredom, it had to be boredom. Longstreet's boots crunched the roadbed, crossing the tracks on the way into town. Long purple shadows crawled down First Street from the last rays of sunset turning the ragged western horizon crimson. He clumped up the boardwalk step. A hollow wooden drumbeat followed his reflection in the shop windows as he passed.

It had to be boredom. What else could it be? Beau Longstreet could have his pick of beautiful women from Charleston to Saint Louis, refined women, genteel women. So why did he find himself drawn to a soiled dove workin' a dump like the Rusty Spike in a shit hole like Julesburg? It had to be boredom. He paused at the bat wings. His aristocratic Southern upbringing barred the entry. Time was he walked down to the slave quarters on the family plantation with fewer feelings of guilt than this. This was different. He was young then. He wasn't a bundle of adolescent longings anymore. Hell he didn't even feel much of an itch now. No, it was something else. Something he'd seen behind her eyes. Something he wanted to understand. He pushed his way inside.

He crossed the bar, instantly aware of her sitting at the back corner table. The smell of stale beer, tobacco smoke, sawdust and the oily scent of kerosene mingled in the dim light, a strong reminder of the shabby condition of the place. The portly bartender with the waxed mustache greeted him with a *what'll it be* lift of an eyebrow, his soiled apron only more so since his last visit.

"Whiskey, two glasses." He waited. The bottle and glasses arrived. He picked them up and headed for the front corner table with a glance in her direction. She didn't seem to notice. Maybe she wouldn't. Maybe he'd just have a quiet drink and go back to his cot in the depot. He poured a drink.

"Expecting someone?" the question invited, soft and husky.

He looked up and surprised himself with a smile. She smiled too. Small crinkles appeared at the corners of her eyes. Some might take them for age. He saw them for amusement that comes with a knowing for life. "I am if you'll join me."

She smiled again and drew back the chair beside him. A faint clean scent of lavender muted unpleasant saloon odors. A low-cut green gown suited the color of her hair. It brought out the golden fleck in her green eyes. Funny, for all the fascination he'd found in them the other night, the color had never registered with him.

She lifted her glass. He touched the rim to his. She held his eyes and took a swallow.

"More questions about Collins and Heffridge?" Her eye sparkled with a mischievous twinkle.

He shook his head.

"Why then whatever brings you back to a place like this?"

He thought, uncertain how to answer, feeling a little tongue-tied.

"You don't really need a reason. I'm glad you're here."

He knocked back his drink and poured another. The whiskey warmed his belly, bolstering his resolve. "Somethin' I saw the other night made me curious, I guess. Course it's none of my business."

"What's none of your business?"

"How a woman like you wound up here, in a place like this."

"You mean how a woman like me wound up a whore?"

"I, well, no, I wouldn't put it like that."

"Course you wouldn't." She patted his cheek. "You're too damn nice, but that's what you mean."

He met her eyes. She bit her lip, considering how much to expose. As a rule she didn't. Beau Longstreet was different. She dropped her lashes, creamy breasts swelled with a sigh. She knocked back her drink and held out her glass. He poured.

"My husband died back in Missouri. I lost the farm. After that, I drifted west. Thought I might find work in the end-of-track construction camps. Barely kept myself fed doin' laundry, mending and such that first winter. Next thing I knew I found myself in Julesburg, hungry and in need of a roof over my head. Somewhere along the way I lost my self-respect. The railroad men had money and needs. It seemed like an easy enough trade. It's better than starvin' or freezin' to death, most of the time."

A solitary tear trickled down her cheek. She looked up eyes brimming. She sighed again. "There, is that what you wanted? Now look what you've done, ruined my makeup sure enough."

He held her eyes unable to answer.

"My turn. Why on earth would you care to know?"

"It struck me you didn't belong here."

She bit her lower lip, staring off into the smoky glow of a kerosene lamp. "Time was I thought the same thing. I haven't thought that way in quite some time. I guess maybe I don't believe it anymore."

"Maybe you should."

"And maybe you're Prince Charming and I'm a Fairy Princess."

She leaned across the table and kissed him, soft and sweet. Something passed between them, something strong. She felt it too.

She lifted her lips from his, her expression oddly confused.

She sat back and wiped the moisture from her eyes in hope of restoring her composure. "You have made a mess of me."

"I'm sorry."

"Don't be. It was sweet, even if it was just curiosity. You know what they say about curiosity." She smiled.

He smiled, tossed off his drink and poured another.

"So what brings a handsome Southern gentleman to the Pinkerton agency and an end-of-track stop like Julesburg?"

"Turn about fair play?"

"It is."

"The war I suppose. We lost. The family lost the plantation. Kind of like you losing the farm. I drifted west too. Went to work for Pinkerton to feed myself and put a roof over my head. Sound familiar?" She favored him with an understanding look he couldn't describe beyond the echoed feeling of her kiss. "One thing led to another. Pinkerton gave me more responsibility. Then somebody robbed a train at Big Springs."

"Now I'm curious. What brought you here, now? When you walked in here and looked my way, I figured you for a man in need of a whore. Now I'm not sure."

They sat quietly for a time, connected by some unseen bond. They shared the same story written in different circumstances, one for a man the other for a woman.

"I asked myself something like that walking over here. To tell the truth, I'm not sure why I came or what I expected to find when I got here. The other night left me with something more I wanted to know. I guess I wanted to know you."

She lowered her lashes and clasped her hands in her lap. An innocent widow from Missouri sat in the midst of a rundown saloon, in a dress that made no secret of her sex. She squared her shoulders and met his eyes. "Did you find what you came for?"

The question might have had an edge. Still it felt soft and

warm in his thoughts. He reached across the table and took her chin in his hand. He drew her lips to his, holding a mystical connection both strong and delicate. He could feel her breath mingle with his. His lips touched hers. A spark jumped between them. It flared, white hot in an instant. She covered his hand on her cheek with hers. She squeezed it and rose.

She led him by the hand to the narrow stairway at the back of the saloon, an unremarkable act in the presence of the usual crowd. He followed her up the stairs. Creaking boards heralded the ascent, his every sense alert, raw, exposed. She led him to a room. Her room he guessed. She scratched a match and lit a single oil lamp on a small table cracked and stained. The room was small and spare, a bed, a chair, a dark window. Dresses and women's things hung on hooks. He'd seen bigger jail cells. She trimmed the lamp, the light softened. She turned to him, her body heat close in the small space. She lifted her lips to his.

Her kiss ignited liquid fire. Lamplight flared a blinding red haze behind his eyelids. Soft swells, round curves, the crinkle of fabric assaulted his senses. He drew back, measuring his want to her need.

She looked up, misty-eyed, sensing the difference in him. The soft glow of lamplight played light and shadow in her hair. He kissed the salty wetness at the corners of her eyes. He fumbled at her back, his fingers clumsy, groping at the fastenings. She nibbled his lip, a small voice caught breathless at the back of her throat. Green satin slipped. His fingertips found the silken curve of her back.

She slipped his coat off his shoulders. His hungry hands left her long enough for it to fall to the floor. She picked his shirt buttons open one by one. He held her taut and warm against his chest. Laces and wriggles, more buttons and boots, he gathered her in his arms. She encircled his neck.

He kissed her with a gentle urgency unknown in her experience with men. He laid her on the bed, bathed in soft light. He paused to drink his fill. A quiver of anticipation thrilled her. A pulse throbbed at her throat. She'd never thought a man beautiful before. They'd bared their souls. She'd never known nakedness so complete. He crawled onto the bed beside her, his touch soft and gentle. He bent his lips to hers. Her breath caught. He'd touched something deep inside. *Oh, yes!* Something she wanted him to know.

Buffalo Station

Bass turned out in the lobby at six o'clock, bathed, barbered and brushed in clean linen. Abby Stone appeared moments later wearing that smile that said she was privately amused.

"Mr. Bass."

He shook his head. "Remember, it's Sam."

"Very well, Sam." She took his arm.

He had the odd sense he was the one being led across the dusty street through the gathering shadows of early evening. The half-curtained window proclaimed *Delmonico's* lettered in gold. Inside candlelit tables set the room off in a warm golden glow. Each table was set with fine china plates, silver and crystal. The waiter, a small man in a frock coat nodded.

"Good evening, Mrs. Stone. Your usual table?"

"If you please, Alanzo."

He directed them to a back corner. He held her chair. "Would you care to see the wine list?" The question was directed to her.

"That would be fine, unless Sam would like something stronger."

Whiskey sounded good. "Wine will be fine."

"Very good." The waiter bustled away.

"Come here often?"

She smiled. "I do. I hope you don't feel slighted by Alanzo catering to your female companion."

"Me? No never."

"Some men might."

The waiter returned with menus and a wine list. He handed the wine list to her.

"The special this evening is chicken cacciatore." He glanced at Bass. "Our steaks are always special."

"They are, Sam. I'll have my usual."

"Very good, Mrs. Stone. Sir?"

"I'll have the same."

"And bring us a bottle of Bordeaux."

"Very good." He disappeared.

"He called you Mrs. Stone. Are you married?"

She arched one brow. "Does it matter?"

"It might."

"Good. Widowed actually."

"I'm sorry."

"Don't be. I'm quite used to it by now. Besides I rather like running the hotel my way."

"You own the hotel?"

"I do."

The waiter returned with wineglasses and a bottle he opened and poured.

She lifted her glass. "To pleasant company."

He touched his to the rim of hers. A delicate tinkle followed.

"So tell me Sam Bass, what brings you to Buffalo Station?"

He thought fast. "I'm on my way back to Texas. I've been visiting my brother in Cheyenne for the past couple of months."

"What do you do back in Texas?"

"Cattle. I took a herd up to Dodge last spring. Once I sold it, I caught a train to Cheyenne for a visit."

"So how long do you plan to stay with us?"

"That depends."

She met his eyes. "Depends on what?"

"All those things you say Buffalo Station has to offer."

"Touché."

The steaks rescued the conversation. He had to allow Delmonico's served a passing fair steak though he might not have fully appreciated it for preoccupation with the woman across the candlelit table. Abby Stone was a stunning woman with a bright mind, ready wit and a self-assured bearing he found quite amazing even by his considerable experience with women. They finished the bottle of wine over pleasant conversation and dinner. She assumed a more traditional female posture when the check arrived. He paid with a bright new double eagle.

She lifted her chin. "Cattle business must be good."

He wouldn't be surprised if she guessed where it came from. "Business can always be better."

"It surely can."

She took his arm on the walk back across the street. The night man dozed on a stool behind the counter. She paused, appraising Bass as she might inspect a horse offered at auction.

"I had a wonderful evening."

"As did I. It seems Buffalo Station indeed has much to offer."

Her lashes drifted lower. "You think so?"

"I do." The silence grew awkward.

She tipped up on her toes and kissed his cheek, turned and disappeared down a darkened corridor.

He stood there for a moment dumbstruck. Shook his head with a shrug and climbed the stairs to room four.

He lit the bedside lamp and trimmed the wick. He'd shed his coat and shirt when the knock sounded at the door. *Now what?*

"Who is it?"

No answer.

He drew his gun on instinct. *The law?* It couldn't be. Could it?

Another knock.

"All right, I'm coming." He opened the door.

She stood there holding glasses and a whiskey bottle. "I thought you might like a nightcap."

He stepped back and holstered his gun.

She glanced at it with that knowing smile. "Jumpy are we?"

He closed the door behind her.

She set the glasses on the side table and poured. She handed him a glass and lifted hers. "To tonight."

He touched her rim and downed his drink. She took his glass, set it beside hers on the side table and turned into his arms.

"You are full of surprises, Mrs. Stone."

"Oh, please." She took charge of his buttons.

ELEVEN

Big Springs, Nebraska

The trail broke away from the rail line headed southeast. Cane reckoned they were about a mile west of Big Springs. The tracks were fresher now. He was gaining on them. It struck him as an odd place to turn south if they were truly changing direction. More likely they were skirting Big Springs. That made sense. Sooner or later they'd need supplies. Skipping Big Springs made Buffalo Station a good bet. The distant whine of a train whistle called the wager. Cane spurred his horse into a gallop down the tracks to Big Springs. Thirty minutes later a stockman loaded a lathered Smoke into a stock car for the run to Buffalo Station.

Buffalo Station

The train steamed east. The rhythm of the rails accompanied the green-gold rush of Nebraska plains beyond the dust-streaked coach window. Cane sat at the back of the car. The few passengers forward of his seat dozed, or read or spoke quietly with seatmates. Collins and Heffridge were out there somewhere. This gamble would either head them off or lose their trail for good. His chances of picking up Bass's trail also hung in the balance. The big fish in his search, Bass somehow managed to slip away. Cane's best hope of picking up his trail rested on the possibility that he and Collins had a plan to meet somewhere. All in all he'd staked a big bet on this train ride. He'd better be right. His gut told him he had one chance.

Julesburg

A sage ball blew out of the northwest on a swirl of dust, bouncing across the tracks ahead of her. She held the red checked napkin, covering the hamper to keep it from blowing away. He might be the most decent man she'd ever met, well beyond the station of a soiled dove. She had no airs as to that. She had no girlish sentiment where men were concerned. Men like Cross took their women however they wanted because they could. Who was to stop them? No woman was worth the gamble. Longstreet admitted he didn't know who Cross was when he stepped in front of him. He did it out of a gentlemanly sense of honor. A rare quality, she marveled, heroic really. She was grateful for it, grateful and more.

She'd truly been surprised when he showed up at the Rusty Spike looking for her. She'd been even more surprised by his intentions. The whole evening became the stuff of fairy tales. A handsome, refined gentleman saw her for something more than a whore. He made love to her like a woman. She'd never really experienced that before. Her husband had loved her, but he'd been a simple farmer, more intent on breeding than pleasure, at least when it came to her pleasure. For all the others it was an act. Something hollow and meaningless she endured, even suffered for a fee.

Beau Longstreet made her something she'd forgotten she could be. He changed her taste for the work she needed to do. Damn him! He'd made a mess of more than her makeup. He hadn't changed her need to work. He'd offered her a gold double eagle. She hesitated, but she'd accepted it in the end. Winter would be here soon enough. Beau Longstreet would be gone long before that. She had no illusions as to that. Still he had her acting like a schoolgirl. He didn't seem to mind her bringing him lunch. On a day like today they might sit on the station platform to eat and talk. Talk without the bawdy edge that accompanied sex for hire. It passed a pleasant hour for her. For Beau, well maybe it just broke the monotony of another tedious day.

She climbed the step to the station platform. Her shoe heels clipped the planks as she crossed to the depot door. She took no note of the dark figure watching from the shadow of the blacksmith shop across the tracks at the edge of town.

Longstreet turned to the sound of the depot door. He pushed his chair back from the small desk and smiled. He eyed the hamper. "You surely are going to spoil me Miss Sadie."

She returned his smile. "How many times must I tell you Sadie will do?"

"Sorry Sadie, old habit I guess."

"Gentleman to a fault I'd call it. Hope you like fried chicken."

"A taste of home fit for Sunday dinner. What a pleasant surprise for lunch on a Tuesday. You do know the way to a man's heart."

"That'll be the day. Now let's eat your lunch before it gets cold."

He took her arm and led her out to the platform. They sat on the east edge, putting the wind to their backs. He watched the wind play at tendrils of rich auburn hair.

She felt his eyes on her. An involuntary little pulse hammered at her throat. Her fingers trembled as she unwrapped fried chicken, biscuits, two cups and a jar of cool tea. She hoped he didn't notice.

"Behold a feast fit for a king!"

She lowered her lashes and shook her head, pleased. "You do go on Mr. Longstreet."

"I believe that should be Beau."

"Dare I dream?"

They both laughed. Neither noticed the lone rider headed toward the depot from town.

Cross's cuts were healing. The bruises had faded some. His rage had not. He meant to kill the Pinkerton son of a bitch. The sight of him with the whore fanned his anger like salt in his wounds. He lifted the hammer thong and eased his pistol out of the holster. He let the gun hang at his side as he approached the tracks at the west end of the platform. Light knee pressure guided his horse along the tracks at a slow walk. The horse stopped at twenty-five paces as if understanding his rider's intent.

Sadie felt it. She glanced over her shoulder. The dark rider silhouetted in sunlight registered instant recognition. "Beau, watch out!" She swung around the platform edge, shielding Longstreet with her body. The gun plumed powder smoke. She never heard the report. The heavy .44 slug slammed into her breast, pitching her back with such a force her body knocked Longstreet off the platform. He drew his .38 from its shoulder holster and rolled under the platform.

The whore lay dead. It served her right. The Pinkerton was nowhere to be seen. "You're a dead man Longstreet." He cocked his gun and nudged his horse forward.

Longstreet lay in dim shadow. Sunlight found its way between the planks in an even pattern marred here and there by chinks in the wood. He fixed on the horse's hooves beyond the maze of platform light and darkness. The beams supporting the platform made narrow channels. He might crawl forward, but the space beneath the beams made it impossible to work his way behind the horse.

"I know you're there, Longstreet. I'm comin' for you."

The horse moved toward the east end of the platform. The pistol shot exploded off to his left, the bullet striking the side of the platform at the depot beyond his left foot. Close. He needed to move. If Cross figured out where he was, he'd have damn few options other than serving target practice. The horse moved.

Cross cut his eyes along the east wall of the depot. *Where the hell is he? Behind the depot, that had to be it.* He eased his horse away from the platform, angling northeast away from anyone hiding north of the east depot wall.

The horse moved, away from the platform, out of sight. Longstreet had the advantage as long as he could see Cross and the gunny couldn't see him. He didn't like losing his edge. Something dark and liquid splashed beside his cheek. Iron wet the musty scent under the platform. Blood. Sadie's blood. Rage flared white hot with memory. He worked his way forward toward the trackside edge of the platform. Hardscrabble dirt and stone-pocked ground scraped his cheek and knuckles. Cross appeared in a chink in the platform. He sat his horse, gun trained on the northeast corner of the depot. Not an easy shot from here. *Could he get out and into firing position before Cross could get off a shot?* He played it in his mind. He couldn't. He clawed his way to the trackside end of the platform and waited.

"Big tough Pinkerton, got a yellow streak fit for a reb. You gonna show yourself, Longstreet, or do I have to come lookin' for you?"

Cross eased his horse north along the east end of the platform.

Longstreet pulled his head and shoulders into sunlight. The air felt fresh in his lungs free of the dusty heat below the platform. He wriggled the rest of the way out and lay flat on his belly beside the platform. He had Cross's back, near the north depot wall. The potential threat wouldn't hold his attention much longer. He needed a real one. The short-barreled pocket pistol wasn't accurate much beyond thirty paces. He needed close range.

He stood, stepped around the platform and began advancing on his target hoping the gunman wouldn't notice. He moved slowly, one eye on Cross and one eye on the ground careful to avoid any sound. Thirty paces. He forced himself to ignore the bloodstained, gingham-clad body lying on the platform. Bitter anger soured in his throat. Twenty paces. They'd cared for each other at some level. Some unknown, mysterious connection bound them. Fifteen paces.

"Drop the gun, Cross."

The gunman froze. The son of a bitch had gotten behind him. A slow smile parted his mustache as he chanced a glance over his shoulder. The Pinkerton stood in plain sight ten paces behind him. Times like these a man had to trust his shot. He swung his .44 on line and fired. The sudden movement startled his horse. The animal sidestepped, sending the bullet wide of the intended body shot.

Longstreet fired. He charged the startled horse, filling his lungs with an old rebel yell called from some long-quiet place. The spooked horse backed and reared, eyes wide, nostrils flared. Cross fought the bit. He cocked his gun and fired wildly.

The Pinkerton caught the gunman's eye at point-blank range. White hot anger blazed in his chest. The pocket pistol spit muzzle flash and powder smoke, round after round slammed into Cross. The first caught him under his extended shooting arm, destroying his aim. The second shattered his hip. The third tore into his rib cage below the heart, pitching him from the saddle.

Longstreet held his aim, waiting for any sign of movement. He stepped closer and rolled the body over with the toe of his boot. Braylin Cross lay dead. He holstered his pistol. He kicked Cross in the jaw, unable to inflict enough injury on the dead man to satisfy his rage. He turned on his heel and walked back to the platform. He sat beside Sadie's body. Dissolved anger choked his throat.

Twelve

Buffalo Station
September 26

A short-long whistle blast roused him from sleep. The train slowed for the roll into Buffalo Station. Minutes passed. A powerful whistle blast, screeching brakes and gouts of steam announced the arrival. The train stopped short of the station to take on water. Cane gazed out the window, sizing up what he could see of the town. Buffalo Station had surely survived more of its end-of-track boom than Big Springs. A small town sprawled around a commercial center north of the depot. Stores and saloons were visible along with a livery and what might be a hotel. If Collins and Heffridge needed supplies, Buffalo Station could more than fill the bill.

Cane shifted on the uncomfortably hard seat, chafing at the delay. He looked across the car to the prairie south of town. Late-afternoon sun slanted out of the west. Not far south of town a wispy cloud of smoke rose to the blue sky just beginning to catch touches of pink. Dust sign and dark smudges suggested some large party making camp. Canc pursed his lips, curious. The train lurched forward slow rolling the short distance to the station platform.

He stood and collected his saddlebags, grateful to be done with the train seat. He made his way up the aisle to the car door as the train lurched to a stop at the depot. He stepped down to the platform. A small rough-cut log depot stood on the far side.

He clumped down the platform steps and walked back to the stock car where a stockman unloaded his horse.

Smoke greeted him with a stomp and a snort, plainly pleased to be done with the rock and sway of the train. He led him to the depot hitch rack and wrapped a rein. He climbed the platform. The door needed a push to break a warped seal. Hinges creaked as he stepped inside the dimly lit office and passenger lounge. The stationmaster, a harried scarecrow of a man with garters holding up his sleeves looked up from a cluttered desk. He blinked owlishly behind smudged spectacles amid a sun washed storm of dust mites.

"What can I do for you?"

"I'm lookin' for the Pinkerton agent."

The little man thumbed toward a shadowed back corner of the passenger lounge. An agent with a drooping mustache sat at a small desk crammed behind the potbelly stove. He snapped out of a doze as Cane approached.

"Pinkerton agent, Reed." He extended a hand. His rumpled brown suit looked as though it had gathered dust with the rest of the place.

"Briscoe Cane."

A flicker of recognition crossed his eye. "Pleased to meet you. I got a wire from Beau Longstreet. He said you might be along."

"Any sign of the men who robbed the train at Big Springs?"

The agent shook his head. "They split up soon as they left town, scattered near as we can tell. From what Longstreet tells me, you got as much trail as anybody."

"I got a hunch two of 'em might be headed this way. Any idea who's makin' camp south of town?"

The Pinkerton nodded. "Fifth Cavalry column headed up to the Powder River troubles. They camp out there to keep the men out of town. Pisses off the saloon keepers and whores somethin' fierce."

"I can imagine. Much obliged for the help."

"You let me know if them two you're after show up."

"You'll be the second to know. Have a good evening."

Shadows gathered as the sun drifted toward the horizon. Cane toed a stirrup and swung into his saddle. He wheeled Smoke south, crossed the tracks and picked up a jog toward the army encampment.

Soldiers milled about the camp or sat taking their evening meal. He'd read the newspaper account of Sherman's plan to confine the hostiles to the reservations this summer. This unit had to be part of that campaign.

A sentry challenge at the perimeter led to the duty officer, a crisp young fellow who likely maintained his commission in the postwar army courtesy of West Point training.

"Lieutenant Benjamin Sparks at your service, sir."

"Briscoe Cane, Lieutenant. I'm on the trail of two men wanted for the Big Springs train robbery. I wonder if any of your patrols might have come across them."

"No reports have come to my attention since I came on duty this evening. Are you an officer of the law?"

"Great Western Detective League." It sounded official. Cane thought it might help.

"I'm not familiar with that."

"We've been retained to recover the stolen gold shipment and bring those responsible to justice."

"I see. It's a civilian matter then. The army can't provide direct assistance you understand. Unofficially you might ask our chief of scouts. His scouting parties might have seen something."

"Unofficially then, where might I find this chief of scouts?"

"The scouts are camped on the west perimeter." He hooked a gauntleted thumb toward a fire site over his right shoulder.

"Much obliged."

He wasn't hard to find.

"Caleb Forrester." The grizzled old scout rose, unfolding his crooked frame from a cross-legged sitting position with an unexpected ease. He wore soiled buckskins and a sweat-stained slouch hat. Clots of gray-streaked hair hung to his shoulders. Deep etched lines hardened his features to a sunbaked mask. His lean jaw jutted behind a scruff gray beard. Watery blue eyes flicked a calculated assessment in his casual greeting. By the look of him he might have been taken for some older unkempt kin to Cane. He stuck out a gnarled hand. "What can I do for you?"

"I'm lookin' for a couple of men. The duty officer thought your scouts might have spotted them."

Forrester scratched his chin. "You the law?"

Cane shook his head. "Bounty hunter."

"Same difference, sit down. I was about to have a bite of supper. T'ain't much, biscuits'n gravy. The cook may have sliced some fatback nearby. Care to join me?"

"Don't mind if I do."

Forrester waved for another plate and returned to his seat beside the fire. The scout camp sprawled away from the regular army camp. Crow and Arikara knotted around their own fires. "What might you be after these men about?"

"It starts with stage robbery and then moves on to train robbery."

"They sound like right upstanding citizens."

The cook, a potbellied man in a stained apron brought him a plate of biscuits ladled with thin gravy. Cane thanked him with a nod. "Last I knew they circled Big Springs headed this way. Did any of your scouts report seeing two men headed this way?"

Forrester shook his head, hocked and spat for emphasis. "Cain't say they did." He squinted off to the southwest. "Then again maybe we just did."

Cane followed the scout's line of sight. At first he didn't see anything but purple haze. Then he made out three dark shapes moving slowly out of the south. "That just might be them now."

"You want some help, just in case?"

"I'd appreciate it."

"It's a civilian matter so you'll have to take the lead. My men and I will back you up if it comes to that."

Cane set his plate aside and headed for his horse. By the time he mounted and rode out of camp, Forrester and a half dozen well-armed men trailed along. As he closed the distance to the approaching riders he made out two of them leading a pack mule.

"Look yonder, Heff." Collins stuck out his chin toward riders approaching in the fading light. "Don't like the look of that." The lead rider picked up a trot closing the distance between them. He drew rein at twenty yards.

"Collins, Heffridge, you're under arrest for the Big Springs train robbery and other offenses."

"Damn!" Collins sighed.

"We could make a run for it."

"These horses are played out. We wouldn't stand a chance."

"What do we do then, give up?"

"You do what you want, Heff. Them sons a bitches ain't lockin' me up."

Cane took the smaller of the two riders silhouetted against the gathering gloom for Collins. He was the one who went for his gun. His shot went wide off the muzzle flash and trailing report. Cane fired twice blinded by his own first flash. He heard a faint grunt. Collins's horse wheeled. Cane's mount danced left as Collins sent another errant shot in the direction he'd just left. Heffridge got off one shot to no effect, when Forrester's scouts lit up the purple dusk with a volley that knocked Heffridge out of his saddle. Cane leveled his gun at Collins. The man fought to control his horse, unable to hold a firing line. Cane's Colt exploded twice. Collins pitched forward beyond the clouds of gray smoke drifting off on the evening breeze. The whole encounter ended as quickly as it began.

Shady Grove

"The next day I received a telegram reporting the conclusion of Cane's pursuit of Collins and Heffridge. Between the two of them he recovered a third of the UP loss. Collins also carried a substantial amount of gold dust that might reasonably be attributed to the Wells Fargo case. Sam Bass and the rest of the loot remained at large."

"That's it for today," Penny said.

I must admit I was so absorbed in the colonel's account I didn't hear her come along when she did.

Crook fished a gold watch from his pocket and popped the lid. "Sure is punctual. You two must have big plans for the weekend." She blushed.

"Can you give us a minute, Penny? Is that the end of the story? I mean Bass was still in Buffalo Station wasn't he?"

"He was. The trail might have ended there for some, but not for Briscoe Cane. That and a little help from a friend, but it appears that'll have to wait until next week."

Julesburg
September 26

Dust swirled behind the dark-suited parson in the wide-brimmed black hat. A handful of headstones, plain wooden crosses and crudely lettered memorials marked the graves of those buried in the overgrown cemetery north of town. Long-street stood at the graveside flanked by the bartender and two black-clad whores from the Rusty Spike.

The parson murmured a familiar passage reading from a well-worn bible. "The Lord is my shepherd, I shall not want . . ."

Longstreet's mind drifted away. She saved his life. He'd enjoyed her company, connected with her in a way he didn't understand and couldn't explain. He'd treated her in a way most men wouldn't. No more than he might have done for any decent woman. Maybe that was it. He'd seen decency where most never bothered to look. In that he may have given her something of value. Something she thought she might never have. She'd saved his life for it. He'd never forget her. It might not be much, but it was more than she had before they met.

Buffalo Station

By the time they reached Delmonico's for dinner the town was abuzz with talk of the shoot-out below the army camp. According to the waiter Alanzo, the Pinkertons claimed they'd gotten two of the men responsible for the Big Springs train robbery. Bass took the news without visible reaction. His mind raced. Suddenly Buffalo Station felt decidedly uncomfortable, the enticing presence of the widow Stone notwithstanding. She ordered wine. He ordered whiskey.

"Can you imagine the nerve of those men? Fugitives from justice ride into Buffalo Station as though they had not a care in the world."

"Hard to believe." He shook his head. "Fortunately responsible law enforcement was up to the task."

"At least they got two of them. Unfortunately the rest of them are yet to be apprehended."

"I shouldn't fret if I were you. Justice is sure to be done in due course."

"One would hope, though I must say I lack your certainty in

the matter. Ah, our steaks are here. I'm ready for more pleasant fare."

By dessert he had a plan. He escorted her back to the hotel and excused himself, feigning illness. Safely in his room he packed his few belongings and let himself out by the back stairs. He collected his horse at the livery and put his plan into action.

THIRTEEN

September 27

Gray morning light seeped through the lace curtains. Cane hadn't even noticed them when he crawled into bed the night before. He slept off the effects of the Collins and Heffridgc pursuit and the showdown it led to. The bright light of day left him with the question of what to do about Bass and the rest of the gang. If he hadn't killed Collins he might have gotten a lead. No time for second-guessing a man in a gunfight. You fought for survival on instinct.

He poured water into a basin on the nightstand and splashed his eyes awake. His stomach reminded him that in all the excitement the night before he hadn't even finished the biscuits and brown water that passed for gravy. He made his way down to the lobby to find the scarecrow night clerk who'd checked him in had been replaced by an attractive auburn-haired woman with a fine complexion.

"Good morning." She favored him with a bright smile.

"Good morning. Might there be a place nearby for a bite of breakfast?"

She lifted her chin toward the door. "Delmonico's across the street."

"Much obliged."

The restaurant came off a cut above the usual frontier fare. Steak, eggs, biscuits and real gravy washed down with a pot of coffee put Cane right to deal with the problem of picking up

Bass's trail. He left Delmonico's and headed for the depot. As expected he was greeted by a telegram from Colonel Crook.

Congratulations on successful pursuit.
UP offers three thousand dollar reward for Bass.
Alert sent to all points.
Return to Denver by first conveyance.

Crook

Return to Denver and what? *Wait?* Wait for what? Wait for the Great Western Detective League to pick up the trail? He crumpled the foolscap. The notion grated on his every instinct as a hunter.

He glanced at the Pinkerton agent hunched over his desk, earnestly discussing some facet of the case with an older gentleman in a bowler hat and tweed jacket. He carried a silver-tipped cane that affected a dandified demeanor amid the rough-hewn furnishings of a frontier depot. The discussion, while animated, appeared casual, lacking the urgency to suggest Pinkerton had anything better to go on than he did. Bass and the others didn't just disappear into thin air. There had to be a trail. He had three thousand more good reasons to find it. Well, eighteen hundred to be exact.

The morning eastbound whistled its approach. Cane stepped out on the platform among a small knot of waiting passengers. A black smoke smudge stained the western sky. Another throaty whistle blast sounded as the engine slow rolled into the station. Her brakes sighed clouds of steam as she drew up beside the platform. Carriage doors opened and disembarking passengers spilled out onto the platform. Further to the west mail and freight made their delivery and departure exchanges. It all appeared routine until Cane noticed a familiar figure among the arriving passengers.

Beau Longstreet stood out in an average-size crowd. He

glanced around and started for the depot. Cane waved him down.

"Longstreet, I didn't expect to see you here. Things must be quiet in Julesburg."

"Not exactly."

"Bass?"

"No. Cross."

"What happened?"

"Like you said, he tried to back shoot me while I was having lunch with Sadie."

"Lunch? I told you she was a grateful whore."

"More than grateful, she saved my life. But please, don't call her that. She's dead."

Cane caught the shadow of grief in Longstreet's eye. "Sorry, I didn't mean no disrespect. What happened?"

"Sadie saw him and warned me. She got in the way of a bullet meant for me. I got to cover and soon enough killed the son of a bitch."

"That what brings you here?"

He shook his head, his thoughts still in Julesburg. "Recalled by the Denver office. Since you're here, I expect that means the Big Springs robbery case is headed this way."

"I got two of 'em last night. The others is still on the loose."

"Any idea who they are or where they're headed?"

"Some. But if we're talkin' information, we're talkin' trade."

"All I know is I was told to report here. I'm to report in with Kingsley."

"Kingsley?"

"Reginald Kingsley heads the Denver Office."

"Reginald?"

"English fella."

"Bowler hat and a tweed jacket?"

"That's him."

"He's in there." He tossed his head at the depot.

"Let me see if we've got any information worth a trade."

"I'm staying at the hotel in town."

Longstreet stepped into the depot lobby amid the bustle of last-minute ticket purchasers, heading out to the train. The measured tones of an English accent colored the soft murmur of conversation coming from across the room.

Reginald Kingsley was unmistakable, though he lacked the look of a Pinkerton operative, much less a master detective and managing director of the Denver Office. He had the pinched appearance of a librarian or college professor with alert blue eyes, delicate features and a full mustache tinged in the barest hint of gray. He favored wool jackets in subdued hues of herringbone and tweed. When called for, he topped himself off in a stylish bowler, properly square to his head. He carried a silver-tipped cane that might be taken for a foppish affectation were it not for the fact that he could wield it as a baton or break it into a rapier-like blade. In the field, he carried a short-barreled .44 Colt pocket pistol cradled in a shoulder holster. He could disappear in a crowd, or turn himself out in a chameleon array of disguises to suit his purposes. He dripped comfortable British charm that easily insinuated itself into the trust of the unsuspecting criminal or better still, criminal informant. Footsteps on the plank floor behind him drew his attention.

"Longstreet old boy, good you're here. Agent Reed here has just been filling me in on the most recent developments in the case."

"I heard we got two of them last night."

"Yes, well I'm afraid it's not quite we. We did recover most of a third of the client's loss. Unfortunately the credit and I'm afraid the reward, goes to a bounty hunter who represents himself to be part of the Great Western Detective League."

"Briscoe Cane."

"Why yes. How did you know?"

"Met him in Julesburg. He helped me out of a little scrape with Braylin Cross."

"You mean to tell me Cross was involved in the Big Springs affair?"

"No. Just a disagreement over . . . over the favor of a lady."
She was a lady.

"A woman, what pray tell did she have to do with the case?"

"She had information on Heffridge and Collins. She'd have claimed the reward on that, as things turned out. Unfortunately they were long gone by the time we got the information."

Kingsley shook his head. "So on top of not bringing that pair to justice, you're telling me we have to pay an informant's reward for information we couldn't use?"

"No need to get yourself in a knot, Mr. Kingsley. I'm not saying that."

"What are you saying then man? Out with it."

"She's dead."

"I see."

"No sir, your thousand-dollar reward is quite safe. She died saving my life. Now unless you've got specific instructions for me, I'd like to get some rest. I've had a tough couple of days."

Kingsley knit his brow, sensing there was more to the young man's story. More that might be best left to himself for the moment. "No, Beau, nothing just now. Get yourself a room at the hotel. You can report here in the morning."

The livery stable was a block down from the depot. It didn't amount to much. A dusty corral and rough-cut barn with a few stalls, a loft and tack room. A ramshackle porch-like attached roof served as a blacksmith shop with its forge, bellows and cross ties. Cane stabled Smoke there the night before. He should have thought of the possibility then, but he didn't. Now he couldn't get the notion out of his head. It wasn't exactly on the way back to the hotel, but it made more sense than waiting around for a westbound train to Cheyenne in the hope Crook's Great Western Detective League would pick up Bass's trail. He found the heavyset figure of the liveryman bent over the hoof of a sturdy buckskin. He let the hoof down and straightened in greeting as Cane approached.

"Come for your horse Mr. Cane?"

"Not yet. More like a curiosity. You haven't by any chance looked after a blue roan in the last week or so?"

"What do you know about that?"

"I'm interested in the man who owns him."

"So am I. He snuck the roan out of here last night without payin' his board."

"What time was that?"

The stableman shrugged. "No tellin'. I turned in sometime after nine o'clock. The horse was here then. He was gone this morning."

Damn it! What the hell had he been thinking last night? "What can you tell me about the owner?"

"Said his name was Bass when he brought the horse in. Said he'd be stayin' at the hotel."

"Any idea where he might have gone?"

He shook dark soot-stained beard stubble. "Wish I knew. I got an unsettled account with him."

"Much obliged." He'd been here as recently as yesterday. Somebody must know where he went.

Abby Stone was miffed, not surprised, but miffed. Men like Sam Bass were the ones who could fool you. Fool is right, disappeared in the night like a bad dream after complaining of a headache. Something didn't feel right about that at the time.

She should have been more suspicious. Cattle sales seldom concluded in mint-new double eagles. Then there was this sudden illness that afflicted him right after they heard about the shoot-out south of town. Capturing two of the men involved in the Big Springs robbery right here in Buffalo Station might make a man uncomfortable if those men could possibly identify him. No chance of that happening. Both of them were dead, but nobody knew that when the news broke at Delmonico's. If that possibility made a man nervous the only safe bet was to run. That would explain his disappearance. Too bad, he'd been entertaining while it lasted. Then again it would have come to an end sooner or later. It always did. The lobby door swung open. *Now what do we have here?*

"May I help you?"

"I need a room."

She opened the register. Big strapping specimen, handsome too, he looked tired for all that. She read his entry. "Welcome to Buffalo Station Mr. Longstreet. Now there's a name with a famous ring to it. Confederate general as I recall."

"My cousin, ma'am."

"Ma'am? Please." She flashed a bright white smile and extended her hand. "Abby Stone."

"Beau Longstreet, pleased to meet you, Mrs. Stone."

"I didn't think you looked old enough to be a general."

"No ma'am, never made more than captain."

"There's that stuffy old 'ma'am' again. Please call me Abby."

He gave her a sloe-eyed grin. "Then you must call me Beau."

"There that's better." *Beau, hope springs eternal.* "Room three, top of the stairs." She slid the key across the counter. "Let me know if you need anything. Buffalo Station has a lot to offer."

"Much obliged, Abby."

She watched him climb the stairs with undisguised interest. Sam who? Easy come, easy go.

Cane left the livery and headed up the street toward the hotel. He couldn't believe he'd let Bass slip through his fingers like that. Had he planned to meet up with Collins and Heffridge? If he had, the shoot-out tipped him off for sure. That left the same old question. Where did he go? He paused on the corner across from the depot. *If he was Bass, what would he do? Easy enough, he'd put as much distance between himself and the law as he could and do it as fast as possible.* He crossed the street to the depot. He found the stationmaster behind the ticket counter.

"What can I do for you?"

"Did you take on a passenger last night shipping a blue roan?"

He shrugged. "You'd have to ask my night man. He's gone home to bed."

"What time does he come back?"

"Six o'clock. You might ask the stockman. He might know."

"Where do I find him?"

"Stock pens, east of the depot."

Cane touched his hat brim. "Much obliged."

The stockman was more like a stock boy, not quite grown into a gangly rawboned frame. He pushed a battered slouch hat off a shock of unruly brown hair matted with sweat. He wiped his brow on a sleeve.

"Howdy, mister. You shippin' or receivin'?"

"Receivin' a little information I hope. Do you know if a passenger shipped a blue roan last night?"

"Sure, loaded him myself, I did."

"You don't happen to know where he was headed?"

The lad shook his head. "All I know is that he boarded the 10:10 eastbound."

"Well that's more than I knew when I got here. Thanks, son."

116

Cane had enough to pass on to Colonel Crook. He headed for the depot telegraph office. Time to see what the colonel's league could do.

FOURTEEN

Longstreet couldn't say if it was late-afternoon sun or the rumble in his gut that woke him. Likely some of both. No, more likely it was hunger. He hadn't eaten anything since leaving Julesburg. He made his way downstairs. Abby Stone was still at the counter conversing with a thin older gentleman with garters gathered at his shirtsleeves. She brightened at the sight of him.

"You look a bit more rested than when you checked in."

"I am. Now I'm mindful of the need of a meal. Any suggestions?"

"I was just about to head on over to Delmonico's for some supper. Care to join me?"

It was Longstreet's turn to smile. "Best offer I've had all day."

"Probably the only offer you've had all day."

"Might be, I don't rightly recollect."

"Well at least I didn't come in second best." She stepped out from behind the counter and led the way to the door.

"I hope you don't think it forward of me inviting you to supper."

"I'm never put off by the invitation of a beautiful woman."

"Now that's much better than coming in second best." She took his arm as they crossed the street.

The table service and linen told Longstreet Delmonico's was a step up from the usual frontier café. A waiter in a starched white apron smiled in greeting. "Your usual table Mrs. Stone?"

"Thank you, Alanzo."

He showed them to a quiet corner table and held her chair.

"We've a shepherd's pie on special this evening. May I get you something to drink or would you prefer a bottle of Bordeaux?"

"Beau?"

"I take it the wine is your usual."

She nodded with her eyelashes.

"That will be fine."

"Very good, sir." He went off to fetch their wine.

"Come here often?"

"How did you guess?"

They both laughed.

"How's the shepherd's pie?"

"One of my favorites. The steaks are also excellent for a hungry man."

"I am that."

The waiter returned with a bottle and glasses. He poured a small splash for her.

"That will do nicely, Alanzo."

He poured. "Are you ready to order?"

"Beau?"

"I'll have a steak."

"Very good sir. Mrs. Stone?"

"I'll have the special this evening, Alanzo."

He turned on a heel and floated away.

He lifted his glass. "Here's to pleasant company."

She touched the rim of her glass to his and smiled. She took a small sip.

"So Beau Longstreet, what brings you to Buffalo Station?"

"I'm with the Pinkerton agency. We're investigating the Big Springs train robbery."

"And were you involved in that dreadful shooting last night?"

"No, I'm afraid not. That was Briscoe Cane's work."

"Ah yes, Mr. Cane, I believe we have him registered too. And does that finish your work on this case?"

He shook his head. "That accounts for two of them. Three more are still on the loose with most of the money."

"Any idea who they are and where they are headed?"

"We know who they are. If we knew where they were it's likely I wouldn't be sitting here."

Her lashes fluttered. "That would be a pity."

"I'm pleased you think so."

"One of the men you're after wouldn't happen to be Sam Bass would he?"

Longstreet's jaw dropped. "Why yes. How did you know?"

"Just a lucky guess. He sat in that very chair last night. He disappeared right after the shoot-out. I suspect he lit out like a puppy with his tail on fire."

The waiter arrived with their meals.

Longstreet eyed his steak. "That looks good."

"It is. Buffalo Station has a great many good things to offer."

"I see that."

She held his eyes.

"Just one more question?"

"Just one?"

"I mean one more about Sam Bass. You wouldn't happen to know where he went would you?"

"He said he was on his way to Texas."

"Texas is a big place."

"Best I can do."

"I'm sure there's a great deal you do better than just that."

"If you don't run straight off to Texas, I'm sure we can find something."

Her lashes fluttered again.

Bass caught the 10:10 train east, that much Cane knew. How far he went and where it might lead were questions left unanswered. Cane couldn't think them through on an empty stomach. He ran into Longstreet and the woman from the hotel returning from supper as he left the hotel for Delmonico's. Longstreet didn't let any grass grow under his feet, or so it seemed. He touched the brim of his hat as they passed.

"Ma'am, Longstreet."

"Evenin' Cane. May I present Abby Stone."

"Mrs. Stone, my pleasure." He turned to Longstreet. "You come up with anything worth tradin'?"

"Maybe so. Did you come up with anything?"

"Maybe so. You want to have a drink and compare notes?"

Longstreet glanced at Abby Stone. "I'm ah, busy at the moment."

"I can see that."

"I'm to report to Mr. Kingsley in the morning. Why don't you stop by the depot? I'll introduce you to him and maybe we can do some business."

"Sure. See you then. Have a pleasant evening."

September 28

Longstreet eased out of bed so as not to disturb her rhythmic breathing. Morning sun seeped through the curtains glazing the room in a tawny glow. He rummaged among the hastily discarded piles of clothing, piecing together those that were his. It had been quite a night. Abby Stone had the body of a goddess, the appetites of a whore and a sharp wit to top off the whole package. He tiptoed out the bedroom door to the small parlor at the front of her rooms. He pulled on his pants and sat on a velvet tufted chair to contemplate his boots. She'd suggested a drink after dinner. The crystal decanter sat innocently on the sideboard where they'd left it. Two glasses stood abandoned on a table beside the settee. That's where it all started. A drink, a little conversation and what began as a simple good-night kiss.

He pulled on his boots and stood to tuck in his shirt. He had no idea what time they'd finally given in to sleep. Not long ago, judging the weight of the night's exertions he carried. He picked his coat off the back of the chair.

"You running off to Texas without saying good-bye?"

She stood in the bedroom door, wrapped in a sheet. Soft light lit embers of warmth aglow in her beautifully disheveled hair.

"Never without saying good-bye, but I must report to work."

Her lip turned out in a pretty pout. What man could resist that? Two steps and he had her in his arms. Her mouth welcomed his. Possibilities and promises exchanged unspoken.

"I'll be back."

"Promise?"

"I'll be back." He crossed the small parlor to the door.

"I'll be waiting."

He turned.

The sheet slipped.

FIFTEEN

Longstreet strolled across the depot platform, squinting against early-morning sun bright and low in the east. He paused inside the depot allowing his eyes to adjust to shadows muted by window grime. Kingsley sat at Agent Reed's cramped desk, nursing a steaming cup of tea.

"Longstreet, I say you're looking more like your old self this morning. Ready to take on the challenges of the day are we?"

"Ready as I'll ever be. Any new developments overnight?"

"A couple of reports so far, you can read at your leisure. Nothing of substance I fear."

"I have something."

Kingsley lifted the monocle he wore on a velvet ribbon and fitted it to his eye, a gesture he reserved for confronting dubious information. "Have a dream did we?"

"No sir. I had dinner with a lady who had information that may prove relevant."

"A lady, you do have a knack for that. How does one find female dinner companionship whilst sleeping off the rigors of a day's travel?"

"Just lucky I guess."

"Yes, quite I'm sure. And what morsel of information might she have had?"

"She says Sam Bass is headed for Texas."

"How might she have come to know that?"

"Bass was a guest in her hotel. He disappeared after the

shoot-out two nights ago."

"Anything else?"

He shook his head.

"Texas is a big place."

"I mentioned that. She said Texas was the best she could do."

At least as far as Sam Bass was concerned.

"Then I suppose that will have to do."

Oh, it did do. "Maybe not."

"There's more? You said Texas was all she had."

"Briscoe Cane may have more."

"Cane again. What's he done this time?"

"I'm not sure. He may have more information. We discussed a trade."

"A trade?"

"Yes compare notes. We tell him what we know. He tells us what he knows."

The Englishman stirred his creamed tea in thought. "The whole is greater than the sum of its parts is it? Can we trust him?"

"I'd say so, at least so far as the trade is concerned. After that it's every man for himself."

"When might we have this exchange?"

"I asked him to come by this morning to meet you." He lifted his chin toward Kingsley's teacup. "Now is there any chance I might find a cup of coffee around here?"

Kingsley tapped his cane on the floor and tipped the silver knob toward the stove.

"You'll find a pot and cups there. Can't imagine how you colonials abide the wretched stuff."

Cane had a hot breakfast and a leisurely stroll down to the depot. An early taste of autumn chill freshened the morning breeze on a bright sunny day. He found Longstreet and the

Englishman sitting around the Pinkerton desk in the passenger lounge. Both rose to greet him.

"Good morning, Briscoe," Longstreet said.

"Beau." He eyed the Englishman.

"May I present Reginald Kingsley."

"Mr. Kingsley, Briscoe Cane."

"My pleasure, Mr. Cane. I've heard a great deal about you."

"Most of it legal I hope."

The Englishman chuckled. "No outstanding warrants or dodgers so far as I can determine at this hour."

"We can thank the good Lord for that."

"Have a seat." He indicated a chair beside the desk.

"Beau here tells me we may have a mutually beneficial exchange of information in regard to the Big Springs train robbery."

"We discussed the possibility."

"As you know Pinkerton has been retained to recover the lost gold shipment and bring to justice those responsible for the loss."

"As I recall Union Pacific retained Pinkerton to prevent the loss in the first place."

"Yes well, to put a fine point on it that may be true, but not germane to the present discussion. What is your interest in the case?"

"I'm a bounty hunter. I work for the Great Western Detective League. They've been 'retained,' to use your term, by Wells Fargo to recover the proceeds of a Cheyenne & Deadwood stage robbery. The men responsible for that robbery were also involved in the Big Springs robbery. I got one of them two nights ago along with one of the train robbers."

"Yes, I'm aware of that. You're to be congratulated."

"Thank you. The other man I'm after is Sam Bass. He's the brains behind both robberies. That explains why we're here.

The question is what happened to Bass?"

"We believe he was here."

"I know he was here. I'm prepared to put what I know on the table. Are you prepared to do the same?"

Kingsley looked at Beau and nodded. "How do you know he was here?"

"Bass rides a blue roan. He stabled it over at the livery until two nights ago."

"The night of the shoot-out, that squares with what we know. He checked out of the hotel two nights ago. Do you have anything further?"

Cane nodded. "Do you?"

Kingsley nodded.

"Bass took the 10:10 eastbound the night he left town."

"That makes sense. He had to get far away fast."

"It still doesn't tell us where he's headed. What else have you got?"

Kingsley glanced at Longstreet. "He's headed south."

Longstreet blinked.

"How do you know?" Cane said.

"Beau heard it from a woman who had knowledge of his intentions."

Cane could guess who that might be. "So that's it. He's headed south. That covers a lot of territory."

"It does."

Longstreet looked at his boots.

Cane cut his eyes from Beau to the Englishman. "Well south is better than he could be anywhere." He pushed back his chair and rose. "Gentlemen, good luck." He turned on his heel and left.

Longstreet fixed Kingsley's gaze. "You didn't tell him. Why?"

"You said it yourself, old boy, it's every man for himself."

★ ★ ★ ★ ★

The boardwalk ran out at Central Avenue. Cane sauntered up the street following the directions he'd been given by the hotel clerk. He found the Alhambra Saloon a block north of Buffalo Station's main street and two blocks east of the depot, not exactly the commercial center of town. The Alhambra didn't live up to its highbrow handle even in the gloom of early evening. It was a run-down, backstreet hole in the wall. It didn't look like Longstreet's style, which had him wondering why the Pinkerton man had left a note at the hotel to meet him here. He paused at the bat wings to check his guns and blades. Places like this could be full of surprises. He eyed the matched doors. The one on the left looked like it might come off its hinges. He eased through the right side. The place smelled of stale tobacco smoke, beer and a clientele that wasn't partial to washing in any of its accepted forms. The place got a low light glow from a scattering of kerosene lamps that added inky soot stains to the dilapidated atmosphere.

He glanced around the bar. Longstreet sat at a back corner table. A couple of rough types sat at another table. Another stood at the bar, talking quietly with the bartender. The bartender lifted a suspicious brow at Cane. Longstreet had a bottle and glasses. He headed for the table and a chair that put his back to the wall.

"Nice place. You ever consider meetin' in a privy?"

"It serves a purpose. Have a drink. It'll take the edge off."

"Lye soap and a coat of paint wouldn't take the edge off this place."

"Try the whiskey. It's quicker."

Cane poured a drink, tossed it off and refilled his glass. "So what's the useful purpose for meeting in this dump?"

"There's no chance Kingsley or anybody else from Pinkerton is gonna see us."

"Interesting. What's so secretive?"

"Kingsley didn't play straight with you."

"No? Can't say I'm surprised. How so?"

"Bass is headed south all right, south to Texas."

"That narrows the search some. Still Texas is a big place."

"That's what I said, but at least we've got a fair trade now."

"Why tell me? You work for Pinkerton. If Pinkerton gets him you come out ahead."

"Some see it that way. We made a deal. I don't hold with cheating."

Cane lifted his glass. "You're a stand-up guy, Beau Longstreet. I spotted that when you stepped in front of Braylin Cross."

"Thanks."

"If you feel that way, tell me why you work for these guys."

"They offered me a job when I needed one. They've been fair with me. Work is steady. The paychecks are regular."

"You could do better."

"What do you mean?"

"You could make more money workin' for yourself, like me."

"Like you? I thought you worked for that detective league."

"I take assignments from them, but I work for myself. If you get Bass, what do you get from Pinkerton?"

"I'm not sure I know what you mean."

"Let me guess. If you get Bass, you'll get your pay, a pat on the back maybe and a new assignment."

"So?"

"Pinkerton gets the reward."

"Yeah, so?"

"If I get Bass, I get fifteen hundred dollars of the reward money. I'll collect sixty percent of the reward for Collins and Heffridge. The league gets seven hundred. That's the difference."

"That is better than a pat on the back. You think this detective league of yours would take me on?"

"They might. I'd put in a word for you with Colonel Crook. Think about it. If you want to take a kick at the can, you can reach me through the Great Western Detective League Denver Office."

"You headin' off to Texas or back to Denver?"

"That's up to Colonel Crook. If it was up to me, I'd be goin' to Texas. Like you said Texas is a big place. Chances of me findin' him would be slim. The way the league works Crook will put out a notice to his operatives to be on the lookout for Bass. Sooner or later, he'll turn up. When he does, we move in. Until then, I guess I'll be headed back to Denver."

"So this league of yours is like Pinkerton except the operatives take the biggest share of their work."

"That's about it. I'm pretty new at it. Bass and Collins were my first case, but from what I can see now this makes more sense than hunting bounty on my own."

"I'll think about it."

"Good. Now tell me about Mrs. Stone."

He met Cane with a blank expression. "A man who don't cheat, don't kiss and tell either. Now if you'll excuse me, I have a promise to keep."

Cane laughed and threw back his drink. "Nothin' I admire more than a man of his word."

Buffalo Station

"Top of the morning, old boy." Kingsley beamed touching the knob of his cane to the brim of his bowler.

"You seem quite pleased with yourself this morning," Longstreet said.

"Yes, I suppose I am. It seems we made a jolly good trade with your friend Mr. Cane. He said he received a telegram from his superiors this morning, recalling him to Denver. He's purchased a one-way ticket to Cheyenne. 'South' isn't much of a trail is it?"

"No, it's not."

"I shall be leaving myself within the hour for Denver. No sense waiting here until we have something further to go on. I want you to arrange travel to Dallas. It is the most logical of a handful of likely destinations Bass might have. We know he has a fondness for gambling. I should think a surveillance of gaming establishments might prove fruitful. Notify me at once should you have any report of him."

Dallas. He could make Abilene by rail, then what? He had a nasty feeling he'd see more stage than rail on the way to Texas. Thinking of Abilene reminded him he'd be saying good-bye to Abby Stone.

Supper at Delmonico's was always pleasant. Abby turned herself out to fine effect in a dark-green dress that set off her hair and eyes against the flawless promise of a porcelain complexion. That would come later. She eyed him thoughtfully across the candlelit table.

"You're leaving aren't you?"

The question caught him off guard. He nodded. "Kingsley's sending me to Dallas. How did you know?"

She smiled a farseeing smile. "Woman's intuition."

"Sorry. I meant to tell you."

"Don't be. We both knew it would happen sooner or later. It's been great fun. And it's not over yet. As they say, the night is still young."

"The night is young."

She laughed a knowing laugh. "Now eat your steak. A man has to keep up . . . his strength."

Shady Grove

The colonel paused as though he might be collecting his thoughts. His head nodded. He snapped awake. I sensed our session coming to an end.

"So why didn't you send Cane to Texas?"

He shook his head. "Sending him to Texas didn't make sense. It would have had him lookin' for a needle in that haystack. We had people in Texas. Sooner or later a man like Bass was bound to turn up. I telegraphed a dodger to our operatives. Information comes to a patient man who keeps his eyes open and an ear to the ground. I've found that to be a sound investigative principle. One you'd do well to remember, Robert."

"Did you recruit Longstreet?"

"Thoughtful fellow that one. We didn't get him right off."

Footfalls sounded on the polished floor. I knew that sound.

"Time for supper, Colonel."

I stood. Penny's eyes twinkled in greeting.

"You two have big plans for this evening?"

She wagged a finger at him in mock admonition. "You wouldn't be prying would you, Colonel?"

"Me? Heavens no, wouldn't think of it." He smiled and patted the bottle under his lap robe with a conspiratorial wink. "See you next week, Robert."

She wheeled him down the hall with that lovely sway I never grew tired of watching.

SIXTEEN

Shady Grove

The following week the colonel was waiting for me in the solarium, as I found the sunny spacious visitor's parlor was more properly known. He glanced around as I took my seat, telegraphing the passing of the empty bottle in exchange for my expected delivery.

"I see we have our priorities in order."

He scowled. "Indulge me, Robert. I don't have the range of amusements available to me as those you avail yourself of."

"Me?"

"She's been insufferable all week. Did you have a spat?"

"Heavens no."

"You mean no or not that you know of. There's a difference you know. The ones you don't know about are the worst kind."

"Did it ever occur to you that you might bring out the insufferable in her?"

"Me? Of course not, I'm the soul of pleasantry and discretion. No I'm afraid it cannot be explained that easily. Truthfully where women are concerned, for the most part, nothing can be explained easily. Well forewarned is forearmed. I suggest you bring flowers."

I must admit the old buzzard had me flustered. What had I done? Nothing. Could that be it? Could nothing be wrong?

He tapped a foot impatiently. "Are we going to get on with the story or not?"

"Yes, I suppose we should." *What could it possibly be?*

"Where were we then?"

I consulted my notes. "You'd sent notices—dodgers, you called them—to your members in Texas and recalled Cane to Denver."

"Ah yes, that's when His Lordship let himself out with Cane."

"His Lordship?"

"Kingsley, I sometimes referred to the arrogant bastard as His Lordship."

"You knew him then."

"Casually in those days, we got better acquainted as time went on. He didn't improve with age."

"Is that because he cheated Cane in the exchange of information?"

"That and more as we came to know of him. He had more chicanery up his sleeve than a minstrel show with disguises and sobriquets to go with all of it."

Buffalo Station

Cane boarded the westbound train for Cheyenne. He found a quiet window seat in the last row of the second last car and settled in. He figured to sleep most of the way to Cheyenne and be rested for the ride down to Denver. He tipped his hat over his eyes and leaned against the thinly padded seat.

"I say Cane old boy, is that you?"

The English accent was unmistakable. He glanced out from under his hat brim.

"Mind if I have a seat?"

He took it without waiting for a reply.

"On our way to Cheyenne or Denver are we?"

So much for sleep. "Denver."

The train lurched forward, beginning a slow roll west.

"I should have thought you might toddle off in search of

133

some sign of Bass's trail."

"South is a big place."

"Quite so, though I should think a chap like Bass will show himself before long. Pinkerton will cast our net accordingly."

"I'm sure you will."

"And the Great Western Detective League?"

"South is a big place."

The train picked up speed. The rhythmic rattle of the rails tugged at Cane's eyelids.

"So you said. Longstreet tells me you were quite helpful in that dustup with Braylin Cross."

Cane lifted his hat brim. "Longstreet handled Cross. All I did was cover his back."

"Yes, well, no small detail with the likes of a chap like Cross."

"Longstreet can take care of himself."

"Point taken. Still we are indebted to you for your assistance. Hopefully we shall find opportunities to assist one another as cases like the Big Springs robbery unfold."

Cane arched a brow. "Like the exchange of meaningful information."

"Something like that. This Great Western Detective League of yours, I'm not familiar with it. It must be useful or a man of your abilities wouldn't subscribe to it."

"It seems useful. You might say I'm giving it a try."

"There's a chap in Denver has something to do with it, Crook I believe. Do you know him?"

"Yes."

"We've met on one or two occasions. Bit of a mystery man to me. What's his part in it?"

"He runs the league."

"May I ask how large the organization is?"

"You can ask. I don't know."

"Curious, you are trying an association with an organization you seem to know very little about."

"I know all I need to."

"And that is?"

Cane let a little irritation slip out from under his mask. "The colonel has good information and he pays well."

"That's it?"

"That's what I said."

"Perhaps we shall talk again when you know a bit more."

"I'll look forward to that. Now if you'll excuse me, Mr. Kingsley, I'd like to get some sleep." He tipped his hat over his eyes.

Denver

Cane rode into town, took a room at the Brown Palace and made his way to Crook's Great Western Detective League office. A rather small, unassuming storefront, it might have served the needs of a small law practice which in a sense was the purpose it served. Cane noted the Western Union telegraph office next door which likely accounted for the location. He found Crook seated at his desk.

"Cane, glad you're back. How was your journey?"

"Fine once I got off the train in Cheyenne."

"Something unpleasant about the train ride?"

"Kingsley insisted on taking up the seat next to me."

"I see. He can be a bit of a pain in the ass."

"None needed on those damn leather benches. He's quite curious about the workings of the Great Western Detective League."

"How much did you tell him?"

"Very little. I don't know much."

"Mores the better, the less he knows."

"Any word on Bass?"

"Not yet. These things take time. He's probably still traveling to Texas. I've alerted league members in the more likely of his destinations. Something is certain to turn up before long."

"That's what Kingsley said."

"The trick is for us to turn him up before they do. I'm pleased you came in. I have something for you." He opened a desk drawer and drew out an envelope he passed across the desk.

Inside Cane found a bank draft made out to him.

"Your share of the Wells Fargo reward for the recovery of Collins's share of their shipment. I trust the amount meets with your approval."

"It'll keep me fed and bed until we get our shot at Bass."

"I thought so. You see information can be quite useful in this line of work."

Cane pocketed the draft. *It can.*

Dodge City, Kansas

Longstreet boarded a stage bound for Dallas. Two days out the ride was hot, dusty and bone weary. The only thing to be said for it was that it gave a man time to think.

Abby Stone.

Now there was a thought to while away some miles. They'd had a fond farewell that didn't allow for much sleep. He took care of that on the train to Dodge. Stage monotony gave him pause to savor the memory of her. Fascinating, brilliant and gorgeous, the mere thought of her stirred his cupidity. And where did that leave him? On a stage to Dallas for the Eye that Never Sleeps.

He was beginning to feel like that eye. Cane got his check and a return to Denver to await developments. He got sent to Dallas in hope of finding a development. He could have as easily awaited developments in the tender embrace of Abby Stone. Oh and then there was the check. Maybe Cane was on to something after all. Well they were both on the case. Time would tell who might come out the winner. Would it be Cane and the

Great Western Detective League or the Eye that Never Sleeps?
Either way, Beau Longstreet didn't figure in much by way of
sleep, let alone the spoils.

SEVENTEEN

Shady Grove

Penny showed no sign of displeasure with me on our Sunday sundae outing. Either whatever may have been bothering her had passed, or the old scoundrel simply enjoyed picking at the tethers of our emotions. In truth I suspected the latter. He was for all else an insufferable tease. She wheeled him into the solarium with her sweet Mona Lisa.

"Good morning, Robert. I see you've mustered the temerity to come back for more, though I'm not sure if it is my engaging company you desire or another excuse to pester the attentions of this young lady."

She rolled her eyes and blushed in the bargain. I liked it. The old reprobate's teasing did offer amusing aspects when I wasn't directly the brunt.

"Of course it's your company, Colonel. I couldn't possibly duplicate your stories in an old newspaper's stuffy archives. They offer black-and-white reports. You on the other hand offer colorful reflections as to be prized by the reader."

"I should hope so, though I dare say I don't believe a word of it." He dismissed the notion with a wave.

"You're welcome to him this morning, Robert."

I nodded my thanks and watched her go.

"You truly are transparent, boy."

"To the practiced eye of an investigator?"

"Investigator yes, but when it comes to that girl you're the one with the practiced eye. How much practice does a man need?"

"Age may have cost you your perspective of that, Colonel."

"Age! Are you suggesting? Never mind. I see your point. My perspective of that practice is a somewhat dim reflection. Now let's see, where were we?"

I glanced at my notes. "All eyes were on Texas."

"Ah yes. It took a couple of months, but sure enough Marshal Stillwell Russell picked up Bass's trail."

Dallas, Texas

Stillwell Russell sat at a cluttered desk in his small office on Houston Street. He read the telegram from Colonel Crook. Both Wells Fargo and the Union Pacific had rewards out for Sam Bass. That made for a high-profile criminal. Russell, US marshal for the Western District of Texas, pulled a frown. The frown came easy to his dour expression. He had long features made the more so by curly muttonchop sideburns. They gave him an appearance crossed between a stiff-necked preacher and a bloodhound. Crook had reason to believe the outlaw was headed for Texas. If he was right, Bass would likely pass through his jurisdiction even if it wasn't his final destination. Reason enough to be on the lookout.

He mulled the question of what being on the lookout might mean. It would be easy enough if Bass pulled a job. The more interesting question was what could be done to spot him before he did. The man's description could have fit half the cowboys, drifters and gunmen in north Texas. Not much help there. Then it hit him. The man was flush with newly minted twenty-dollar gold pieces. Put one of those together with the description and a man might have something. He'd make the rounds of the saloons and whorehouses. Give the bartenders and whores the description of a man who might pay in new gold double eagles.

Offer them a fifty-dollar reward for information leading to the man in question, and he'd have the best eyes and ears a man could ask for on the lookout.

He cracked a half smile, as if to prove he could.

October 1877

You had to get there early. If you waited until the gambler had a game, you could wait a long time for a moment or two of quiet conversation. That's how Longstreet had it figured as he began canvassing the games that dotted Dallas saloons. It didn't take long to turn up new information, even if it wasn't the sort of information he'd bargained for.

He arrived at the Lone Star saloon during the supper hour. He ordered a beer and took a seat at a corner table that gave him a good view of the other tables. The early evening crowd was thin. The real action wouldn't start until later. One beer and thirty minutes after he sat down the man came in. He was turned out in a frock coat and brocade vest. He had a waxed mustache and cold eyes. He took a seat at a table off the far end of the bar facing the door. He produced a deck of cards and began shuffling in the idle manner of a man whiling away the time, waiting for a game. Longstreet took his chance.

The gambler looked up at his approach. "Looking for a game?"

"Information." The scent of pomade rose above the familiar stale saloon smell.

"I deal in cards."

"Information that pays."

The gambler paused his shuffling. A flicker of something crossed his eye as he appraised Longstreet. "What sort of information?"

"I'm looking for a man."

"What's that to me?"

"He likes to play."

"This information, what does it pay?"

"A hundred dollars if you spot him for me."

He glanced around the room. "You the law?"

"Pinkerton. Beau Longstreet." He extended a hand the gambler ignored.

"They call me Cutter. Have a seat."

Longstreet pulled back a chair.

"This man have a name?"

"Sam Bass."

"Let me guess, tall fella, ladies might find handsome. Sports new-minted gold double eagles."

Longstreet sat back. "How'd you know?"

"Popular fella."

"Who else is lookin' for him?"

"US marshal, name of Russell."

"Reward?"

The gambler nodded.

"My offer's better."

The gambler arched a dark brow.

Longstreet thought fast.

"I'll make it better."

"How's that?"

"Two hundred if he comes back to your table in time for me to catch him."

"How am I supposed to arrange that?"

"You strike me as a resourceful fellow. He likes to play. I bet you might even take some of those double eagles in the bargain."

The gambler smiled. "Where do I find you Mr. Longstreet?"

"Windsor Hotel."

"If he shows up, you'll be the first to know."

Murphy Ranch
Denton, Texas
Fall 1877

Bass arrived in north Texas and headed for the Murphy Ranch near Denton. An old friend, Arkansas Johnson worked for the Murphy outfit. He figured Johnson would help him hide out from any pursuit that might have followed him from Nebraska. He hadn't been there much over a week when things started to take shape.

Evening turned the day's heat cool and pleasant. Bass and Johnson sat on the bunkhouse porch having a smoke after supper. Johnson's hawk-like gaze cut south along the road heading into town. He scratched a match and relit his pipe, letting the smoke drift on the evening breeze beneath a drooping mustache.

"What's so interesting?" Bass said.

Johnson lifted his leather-tough chin to the road. A dust cloud boiled out of the hills, rider coming fast.

"You figure that for trouble?"

"A man don't push a horse that hard unless there's a reason."

"Maybe I should slip out of sight."

Johnson bunched bushy brows in a squint. He shook his head. "No need. It's one of ours."

"How the hell can you tell at this distance? It's damn near dark."

"A man don't ride that hard in the dark lessen he knows his road."

"You sure about that?"

"Mostly."

"What if you're wrong?"

"I ain't."

"How do you know?"

"The kid took that sorrel out after a missing horse this morning."

The rider galloped through the ranch gate and headed for the bunkhouse. He slid the blown animal to a stop and jumped down.

"Who lit your tail on fire?" Johnson asked.

The kid looked to be no more than twenty. Thick and powerfully built, he had a fringe of matted hair hanging below his dusty hat brim. He wore a .44 Colt rigged cross draw on his left hip. He cut a wary eye at Bass.

"Who's he?"

"A friend. Sam Bass meet Frank Jackson. Most of us call him Blocky."

Bass nodded.

"Now tell us what lit a fire under your tail feathers that's worth near killin' a fine horse over?"

"I got him."

"Got who?"

"That horse thief."

"What horse thief?"

"The one ran off the dun that went missin'."

"Well if you got him, where is he?"

He glanced at Bass again. "He's dead."

"You kill him?"

The kid nodded.

"Where's the horse?"

The kid shrugged. "He wouldn't tell me. Kept denyin' he done it. I knowd the black son of a bitch was lyin'."

"What black son of a bitch?"

"Henry Goodale."

"How'd it happen?"

"I come on him trailin' the horse. I asked him where he took our horse. He said he didn't know what I was talkin' about. I drew my gun and told him horse thieves get hung in these parts. He said he weren't no horse thief and made like he'd be on his way. I told him stop or I'll shoot. He didn't stop. I shot him."

"You killed him."

"That shot didn't kill him. He said, 'Murderers hang too, even for killin' a black man.' I couldn't very well leave him tellin' who shot him, could I?"

"So you shot him again."

He shook his head. "The sum bitch pissed me off so, I cut his throat."

"That figures to have killed him." Arkansas took his pipe stem from between his stained teeth and spit tobacco juice. "Best cool down that horse Blocky before the boss sees him lookin' like that."

He collected the lathered horse and led it to the corral.

Johnson shook his head. "Ruthless son of a bitch."

"That kid could come in handy one of these days," Bass said.

Hiding out, playing cowboy came with a stiff dose of hard work. It didn't take long for Bass to grow restless. Gathering strays with Arkansas one raw afternoon they paused at a creek to water their horses.

"How much longer do you figure to do this, Arkansas?"

"Do what?"

"Punch cows."

"It's a living."

"You call this living?" His eyes swept rolling fields of treeless dry winter grass and sage cut flat by a chill wind beneath a canopy of rumpled gray cloud. "Where's the fun? I ain't had a woman or a good card game in a month."

"That kind of fun takes money."

"It does. More than a man makes punchin' cows."

"What're you thinkin', Sam?"

"A man would have to punch cows ten years to make as much as the shares we took off that train in Nebraska for the price of a night's work."

He nodded and shifted in his saddle. "It'd take more than two of us to pull off something like that."

"Yup. We could use that kid, Blocky."

"We could. Might convince the Murphy kid to throw in too."

"Jim?"

"Yeah. He's got a wild streak. He'd figure it for a good time."

"Know anybody else reliable?"

"There's a couple of boys over to Denton we could talk to."

"I think maybe we should. My ass is chapped with chasing beeves from dawn to dark."

Alamo Saloon
Denton, Texas

The bottle passed around a cracked table from Johnson to Seaborn Barnes, to Tom Spotswood and back to Bass. Arkansas arranged the meeting with two hard cases down on their luck. He represented the men were reliable and competent.

"Arkansas here says you might have a job for us," Spotswood said.

Bass nodded. "I might. Pay's good. Work's light, for a man willing to take a chance."

"For a man willing to take a chance; or a man willing to cross the line?"

"You could put it that way."

"Pay's right, I'm willing. How about you Seaborn?"

Barnes knocked back his drink and poured another. He favored Spotswood's question with a shrug and a nod.

"What do you have in mind?"

Bass glanced around making sure no one was in earshot. "A train."

Spotswood scratched his chin. "Trains take some know-how."

"Ever hear of the Big Springs robbery?"

"Who hasn't? Union Pacific lost sixty thousand in gold."

"They did. That's why you rob trains."

"That takes care of why. It still takes know-how."

"Who do you think robbed that train?"

Spotswood met his eyes. "You?"

Bass nodded.

"Count us in."

Barnes tossed off his drink.

EIGHTEEN

February 22, 1878

The Texas Central built the watering station that would become Allen, Texas. At the time, it wasn't much more than that, a stop on the track between somewhere and somewhere else. It made a perfect spot for a daylight robbery on a clear chill winter afternoon in north Texas. Engineer Casey Cavanaugh had no more than braked the 6:20 to a stop at the watering station, when masked bandits appeared from behind the depot. A masked-up Seaborn Barnes rode up beside the locomotive and leveled a sawed-off shotgun at his chest.

"Don't move and you won't get hurt. You, fireman get down off that tender where I can see you."

Safer Stringman climbed down, the whites of his eyes bulging against sweat-shined black skin. Further up the train Jim Murphy got the drop on the conductor.

Blocky Jackson and Arkansas Johnson entered the passenger carriages masked-up with guns drawn. Women gasped. Well-dressed gentlemen turned ashen.

"Hands in the air and nobody gets hurt." Johnson waved his gun to make the point.

Jackson produced a flour sack and handed it to a man in the first row. He leveled his gun. "Your wallet, that watch, all of it in the sack."

Wide-eyed the older gentleman did as he was told.

"Now pass it along, just like the collection plate at Sunday services."

Johnson laughed, his gun and his eyes flicking along the car from one passenger to the next. They moved down the aisle systematically relieving passengers of wallets, watches and such other baubles that might prove of value.

In the mail car, Tom Spotswood leveled his gun at the messenger guard. Bass searched the car. He found nothing more than a mail pouch. No mint shipment this time. He threw the pouch onto the roadbed and jumped down after it. Arkansas and Blocky cleared the last passenger car, carrying a flour sack full of loot. Bass waved Murphy and Spotswood off the train. He signaled Barnes to let the train go.

The brake released with a groan. Couplings engaged, a chain reaction clank rippled down the train to the caboose. She slow rolled out of the station, gathering speed. The gang mounted up and lined out for the hills.

Thirty minutes later Bass called a halt to rest the horses and divvy up the loot in a white-oak thicket beside Sweet-Water creek. Spotswood dumped out the flour sack while Johnson rifled the mail sack. Twenty minutes later Spotswood held up a fist full of cash.

"Thirteen hundred dollars and some watches, two hundred and some a man." He spat.

Bass shrugged. "It ain't a mint shipment, but you don't get one of those on every train."

"Whole lot of trouble for two hundred bucks."

"What are you bitchin' about, Tom?" Blocky said. "You punch cows four months for that kind of money."

"Blocky's right," Johnson said. "It's one job. Once you're over the line, you keep going. Sooner or later you catch yourself a big prize."

★ ★ ★ ★ ★

The mail sack didn't yield much loot, but the federal offense got Stillwell Russell on the case officially. He immediately swore in a posse and lit out for Allen. They picked up the gang's trail and tracked them into the hills. They found the white-oak stand at the creek bed where the sign said the gang stopped before splitting up. Other than a discarded flour sack and a mail bag with its contents rifled, they didn't find anything more useful than horse droppings. The lack of tracks leaving the grove suggested most of the gang used the creek to cover their tracks. Russell had his men fan out, riding the creek banks looking for sign. After an hour's search trackers concluded that most of the gang covered their tracks as they left the stream. They found one fresh set of hoofprints, leaving the stream headed southeast deeper into the hill country. The trail petered out a few miles from where it left the stream. Russell called a halt. *Now what?*

Ben Davis, one of the trackers, spoke up. "Marshal, I recollect an abandoned line shack not far from here. Saved my life in a snowstorm some years ago. He might a gone there. It ain't no more'n a hunch, but there it is."

"Best we got at the moment, Ben. Mount up."

Thirty minutes later Davis led them into a blind draw. The shack sat on a low rise, well out of sight. A bay horse slept hip-shot, picketed beside the cabin.

"Looks like we might a struck it lucky," Russell said. "This draw has him boxed in pretty good. Ben you stay here with a couple of the boys in case he gives us trouble. The rest of you, unlimber them guns and follow me."

Russell and his men rode into hailing distance.

"Yo the cabin! US Marshal Stillwell Russell. Come out with your hands up!"

An anxious moment passed, measured in the buzzing of a fly. The cabin door cracked open. Tom Spotswood stepped out blinking back the sunlight, hands in the air.

"What do you want with me, Marshal?"

"Suspicion of robbery." Russell rode up to the cabin and stepped down. "What's your name boy?"

"Spotswood. Tom Spotswood. I don't know nothin' about no train robbery."

He stopped in his tracks. "Did I say train robbery?"

"Well, I, ah, just guessed."

"Keep an eye on him boys while I have a look around." It didn't take long to search the cabin. The place had that dusty, musty deserted smell that infests abandoned buildings. Spotswood hadn't bothered to tidy up the spiders or the armadillo droppings. There wasn't much of anything else in the place except Spotswood's gear. Russell found two hundred sixteen dollars and a gold watch in the saddlebags. He stepped back outside for a lung full of fresh air.

"Kind of a lot of walkin' around money."

"Ain't nothin' agin' carryin' money."

"Not as long as it's yours. Nice watch." He flipped the cover open and read the inscription. "Who's Emerson Fielding?"

Spotswood shrugged.

"How'd you come by his watch?"

"I won it in a poker game."

"Same game you won the cash in?"

He nodded.

"You're one lucky feller, Tom Spotswood. Leastwise you will be if Emerson Fielding didn't have this watch taken from him by the men who held up that Texas Central train over to Allen a couple of days ago. If he did lose it on that train, you're gonna do hard time boy. Now if you was to tell me who was with you when you robbed that train, things might go easier."

Spotswood cut his eyes to the posse and the guns leveled at him. No way out. They had him dead to rights.

"Sam Bass. It was his idea."

Bass. They had a line on him now. Russell narrowed his gaze, boring into Spotswood. "And?"

Spotswood sang like a bird.

Shady Grove

"I got a telegram from Stillwell Russell directly after that. Sam Bass had turned up sure enough. Cane was plenty willing to head down to Dallas to finish the case. I 'spect he'd a gone even if the Texas Central hadn't added another five hundred dollars to the stack of rewards pilin' up for the man."

"Time for lunch, Colonel."

He glanced up at my Mona Lisa. This would be interesting. The old boy had unfinished business he'd want to clear up.

"Always time for something around this place. Can you give us another ten minutes, Penny? We're at an important juncture in the story and I don't want to lose my train of thought."

She made a mock frown. "Five minutes and not a minute more or you'll have me in trouble for bringing you late." She turned on her heel.

Crook watched until she was out of sight. He produced the empty contraband from under his blanket. We made our customary exchange.

"Now tell me about this important juncture before you lose your train of thought."

He arched a shaggy brow in disgust. "Ain't nothin' wrong with my train of thought. It's one of the few things I got that still works like it should. Course round here that's a rarity. You see how easy I bought the time we needed."

"Resourceful as ever, Colonel. See you next week."

The following Saturday I arrived in the sun-washed solarium, fresh with the scent of floor polish. Penny wheeled the colonel down the hall at the stroke of the appointed hour. We exchanged smiles.

"He's yours for the afternoon, Robert."

"Thank you. Has he been behaving himself?"

"After a fashion, as long as you don't expect too much."

"Listen to you two. Who the hell do you think you are? You treat me like a misbehaved child. I'll have you know I take umbrage at such treatment."

"See what I mean?"

"I do. See you later?"

"Of course."

"Must I sit here and listen to you two further your romantic interests? Come along Robert, you have a book to write."

She gave me a Mona Lisa behind the colonel's back and turned to go. I made a show of groping for my pad and pencil as she crossed the room to the hall.

"I'm not fooled, Robert. You can watch her wiggle on your own time. I'm a busy man. Now let's get on with it. Where were we?"

I sat. "You sent Cane to Dallas."

"Ah yes."

March 20

Cane stepped off the eastbound train in Dallas on a warm sunny early-taste-of-spring day. He slung his saddlebags over his shoulder and headed back to the stock car. As he crossed the platform past the depot headlines sprang from the *Dallas Daily Herald*.

Bass Gang hits Texas Central train at Hutchins

Looks like we made it in time for the party after all. The article reported the robbery had taken place two days before. The bandits made off with an undisclosed amount of cash and valuables taken from the passengers. It sounded like small potatoes again.

He collected Smoke from the stockman, tacked him up and walked him up the street toward town. The arrival of the railroads some six years earlier turned Dallas into a thriving agricultural city of some seven thousand. The streets bustled with commerce, mercantile stores, banks, saloons, hotels and restaurants. According to Crook, Marshal Russell was headquartered at the Windsor Hotel. The Windsor wasn't hard to find. It was easily the biggest building in Dallas. He looped Smoke's rein over the rail and climbed the boardwalk to a broad pillared porch, running the length of the building on either side of a double door center entry. The lobby had a quiet library feel to it with red-velvet-covered furnishings. Heavy drapes of the same blood red muted the outside light to a warm glow. He crossed the freshly waxed floor to a registration counter flanked by a sweeping spiral staircase ascending to the upper guest floors. An officious-looking clerk with a waxed mustache, oddly in keeping with the condition of the floor, eyed him suspiciously.

"May I help you?"

"I need a room. I'm also looking for Marshal Stillwell Russell. I understand he's staying here." The man seemed to relax at the mention of the marshal. He spun the register.

"I'm afraid the marshal isn't in at the moment, but you are welcome to leave a message, Mr. . . . ."

"Cane, Briscoe Cane."

"No need to leave a message, Cane. Russell doesn't hold much with detectives." The unsolicited advice came from a familiar voice behind him.

"Longstreet, what are you doing here?"

"Same as you I reckon. You'll be wasting your time with Russell. He won't cooperate with a private detective."

"You mean he won't cooperate with a Pinkerton detective.

He'll cooperate with me."

"What makes you so sure?"

"Great Western Detective League."

"That again? We'll see."

"We shall. Let me stow my gear and let's go find us a bite of lunch and a beer. It's been a while since Buffalo Station. We probably got some catchin' up to do."

The clerk slid a key across the counter. "Room thirty-five, third floor on your right."

"Much obliged."

Longstreet suggested a small café down the block from the hotel, allowing as how the hotel dining room was a mite stuffy. It was also frequented by others working on the Bass Gang case. They pulled up chairs at a corner table with a blue-and-white-checked tablecloth and blue bandannas for napkins. A chalkboard at the door announced a roast beef and mashed potato daily special. They settled on two orders and two beers.

"So how long you been in Dallas?" Cane asked.

"Kingsley sent me down here after Buffalo Station. He spotted agents in Dallas, Houston and Austin figuring Bass would show up somewhere around one of them. I've been watching the gambling action figuring if he did show up, pretty soon he'd be looking for a game."

"And did he?"

"Look for a game? Hell no. If he had we'd a had him by now. First we knew he was back came out after the Allen train robbery. The gang got away with a mail pouch. That got Marshal Russell on the case. His posse ran down one of 'em. Fella by the name of Spotswood. Ever hear of him?"

Cane shook his head. The waiter arrived with their beer. They both took a swallow.

"So this Spotswood identified Bass?"

"He did, along with the rest of the gang. Now my turn, what makes you so sure Russell will cooperate with you? He's been real tightfisted with the case as far as we're concerned. He comes off as the pillar of public service. He puts his place above any private investigator in it for commercial reasons."

"Unless there's a cut of the reward in it for him."

"What are you talkin' about?"

"He's a member of the Great Western Detective League. All the league members share in a portion of the rewards at the end of the year. Kind of holds everyone's interest in cooperation. The league had Russell on the lookout for Bass before he ever lifted a mail pouch."

"Well that sure enough explains things."

"Explains what?"

"I had to offer my gambler informants extra money to get to the front of the line for information on Bass."

"Russell got to 'em first."

"He did."

Cane smiled. "See how this thing works. I'm tellin' you, Beau, you're wastin' your talents workin' for that Pinkerton outfit."

"We'll see who gets Bass."

Two steaming plates of roast beef and mashed potatoes arrived.

"I 'spect we will."

NINETEEN

Cane paid for lunch. He excused himself by telling Longstreet it might be best if he located Marshal Russell on his own. We wouldn't want to inhibit the marshal's inclination to cooperate now would we? Longstreet got the point.

Cane returned to the Windsor. The registration clerk greeted him with a wave on entering the lobby.

"Marshal Russell returned over the lunch hour, sir. I gave him your message. He said to tell you he's gone to the sheriff's office to check on his prisoner. He said I should tell you to meet him there."

"Much obliged. Where do I find the sheriff's office?"

"Just down the street in the next block," he said, indicating the east.

Cane found the sheriff's office as directed. The door creaked open. The office held the sheriff's desk on one side and a deputy's desk on the other. The barred door to the jail opened at the back beside a rifle rack behind the sheriff's desk. A potbellied stove beat back the early spring chill from the corner across from the deputy's desk. The sheriff sat at his desk facing a long-featured man in a frock coat. The sheriff looked up.

"Sheriff John Logan, how can I help you?"

"I'm looking for Marshal Russell."

"You found him." The long-featured man turned in his chair.

"Briscoe Cane." He extended his hand. "Colonel Crook sent me down from Denver."

A flicker of recognition passed Russell's eye. He rose and accepted his hand. "Pleased to meet you. I'll be with you directly." He turned back to the sheriff.

"I like your idea, John. Spotswood's statement implicates young Murphy. Making a sweep of their ranch makes good sense. Bass knows every draw, creek, cave and thicket in the territory. Hiding's not a problem for him. They need supplies though. Hiding out on a friendly ranch makes sense. Get your warrant and put up a posse. I'm ready to ride when you are."

"Come along Cane. We'll head on up to the hotel. We can talk there."

Outside Russell led the way up the boardwalk. "I've been expecting you."

"Got here as quick as I could. It sounds like you've got some leads to follow up."

"We do. Snagging Spotswood was a big help. We mostly know who we're after. Problem is Bass does know the territory. He worked as a freighter when he first came to Texas. So far he's proved pretty damn elusive."

They swung into the hotel lobby. He led the way to the bar, deserted in the middle of the afternoon. "Beer?"

Cane nodded.

Russell signaled the bartender for two. They took a back corner table away from the door.

"What are the chances we get him before anybody else does?"

Russell shrugged. "Your guess is as good as mine. The sheriffs of Denton and Grayson counties are both out after him. So far they haven't had much success, given Bass's aforementioned knowledge of the territory. Pinkerton has men in town."

"Beau Longstreet."

Russell lifted a brow. "How'd you know?"

"I know him. He's a little frustrated you've frozen him out of this."

He chuckled. "Good."

"Beau's all right."

"Didn't say he wasn't. The idea is for us to get Bass first. We've got Spotswood. He spilled his guts so we know more than the others do. Still that comes up short of putting a collar on any of them."

"Tell me about your theory on the Murphy ranch."

"Mostly Sheriff Logan's idea. Spotswood identified old man Murphy's son Jim as one of those involved in the Allen robbery. John's hunch is that Bass and his men are hiding on the Murphy ranch. He figures Jim and the family are looking after their supply needs. Makes as much sense as anything we've got."

"So you squeeze 'em and wait to see if somebody makes a mistake."

"Something like that."

April 4

The Texas & Pacific track approaching the trestle crossing at Eagle Ford rounded a blind curve to a slow rise. The Bass Gang parked a freight wagon across the tracks on the east end of the crossing where she'd have plenty of time to stop. The gang took cover in the rocks where the grade sloped below the roadbed. The passengers and crew wouldn't see them coming until they had the drop on the crew and entered the passenger cars.

She rounded the bend right on time with a throaty hoot on her whistle. Black smoke smudges stained a bright blue sky as she slowed into the climb. The brakes belched white clouds of steam. Steel wheels screeched in sharp complaint. The big locomotive ground to a halt, car couplings clanking first forward then back. The cowcatcher stopped just shy of the wagon.

The steam hadn't cleared when masked gunmen stormed the train, securing the engine, caboose and messenger car while others entered the passenger coaches. The practiced routine ended in minutes with the outlaws vanishing the way they'd come to horses hidden in a wash beneath a thicket of trees. The crew pushed the wagon off the tracks. It rolled and bounced down the embankment, crashed into a boulder and tipped on its side. The wheels were still spinning when the engineer signaled the brakeman to release the brakes. She rolled out over the ford and picked up a highball to her next stop.

This time it was Seaborn Barnes's turn to bitch. The man was sullen and mostly kept to himself or the company of a bottle. Bass considered him impoverished of wit. Even so he could count.

"A hundred dollars. Hell, this ain't much better'n honest labor for all the trouble we take."

"It is a might puny," Jim Murphy said. "What happened to them big gold shipments you's always talkin' about."

"They don't turn up every time. We'll get us one. Pretty soon I reckon."

"You reckon." Barnes spat. "We got posses combin' five counties lookin' for us."

"They ain't caught us yet have they?" Blocky said. "Sam knows what he's doin'."

"Sure he does, pup. You got it all figured out, ain't you. Not even dry behind the ears yet."

A black light descended over Jackson's eyes. His hand drifted toward his gun. "Who you callin' a pup?"

"You, you snivelin' little shit. You want to make a play, go."

Sam's gun sprang to hand cocked. He stepped in front of Barnes. "Shut up! You got a problem with your share? You take it up with me. There's more and better men where you come from."

"I can take care of myself, Sam."

"I know you can, Blocky. I'm savin' this dumb son of a bitch's life if he ain't too stupid to appreciate it."

Barnes's dull gaze stared round-eyed down the muzzle pointed between them. He raised his hands and backed off. "No trouble."

"That goes for you too, Murphy."

"No trouble, Sam. No trouble a'tall."

Dallas

The Western Union messenger peddled his velocipede up to the Windsor Hotel and jumped down. He leaned the ungainly cycle against a front porch post and hurried into the hotel. Telegrams were always in a rush. The desk clerk smiled at the pink-cheeked young man's officious demeanor. *Hard to make that work in knee britches,* he thought.

"Telegram for Marshal Russell."

"You found him, son," Russell said as he and Cane entered the lobby from the dining room. The young man handed Russell an envelope and caught the quarter the marshal tossed in his direction. He was gone to his next errand as quick as he'd come. Russell tore open the telegram.

"Son of a bitch!"

"What is it?" Cane asked.

"Bass and his gang, leastwise they figure it was Bass." He handed the yellow foolscap to the detective league man.

Cane read. "You gonna organize a posse?"

Russell shook his head. "What for? That trail will be two days' cold by the time we catch up to it. I've rode the skin off my ass half over north Texas and what have we got to show for it? We need a trap. I just ain't figured a good one yet."

"Let me know when you do. I might ride out to this Eagle Ford to have a look for myself. You never know when a man like Bass might get sloppy and make a mistake."

"Suit yourself."

★　★　★　★　★

Cane had nearly finished tacking Smoke when Longstreet came into the hotel livery.

"You headed where I think you're headed?"

Cane turned. Sunlight poured through the stable door rendering the Pinkerton a silhouette between the shadowed stalls. "Where's that?"

"Eagle Ford."

"How'd you find out?"

"Denver Office got a wire from the Texas & Pacific."

"Pinkerton's havin' its share of trouble with this bunch."

"Least we're in good company. What do you expect to find out there?"

Cane shrugged. "Anything would be somethin' more than what I'm likely to find sitting on my ass here."

"I got a better idea."

"What's that?"

"Why would I give that up? You and Russell ain't much for cooperation."

"You talkin' another trade?"

He nodded.

"Kingsley agree to that?"

"Kingsley ain't here."

"I can't speak for Russell."

"No matter. He cooperates with you. You cooperate with me. It's all the same."

"All right. What have you got?"

He looked around, making sure no one was within earshot. "There's a big Texas & Pacific gold shipment, leaving Fort Knox on the tenth."

"I suppose Pinkerton's been hired to guard it."

"What makes you think that?"

"How else would you know? Information like that don't get

161

blabbed all over town."

"No, it don't. Then again if it did, it might attract the attention of a man like Bass."

Recognition dawned on Cane. He smiled and stripped Smoke's latigo. No need to ride to Eagle Ford with that plan.

"Why would the Texas & Pacific agree to such a risky trap?"

"They didn't."

Cane pulled a scowl. "Damn it, Longstreet you're talkin' in riddles!"

Shadows couldn't hide the twinkle in his eye.

"There ain't no gold shipment."

Windsor Hotel

Midday sun turned the lobby to a crimson glow. Russell drummed his fingers on the table his long countenance composed in a dour mask. Cane waited patiently.

"I see the merits, but I don't much like it. Why work with private law in suits?"

"You said it yourself. We do it on the merits. It's a good idea. Pinkerton can arrange it. Have you got a better plan?"

He rubbed his chin with a meaty paw. "Not at the moment."

"Half a loaf is better than none."

"So they say. It just sticks in my craw."

"Longstreet didn't have to bring us in on this."

"No he didn't. So why did he? What's in it for him?"

"He's a straight shooter. Likely he'll expect we return the favor somewhere down the road."

"I knew there'd be a catch."

"What catch? As of now Pinkerton holds the best cards. The reward for Bass is substantial. We'd be on the case for half the amount wouldn't we?"

"I s'pose."

"Good. It's settled then."

TWENTY

April 10

Longstreet let word of the gold shipment leak in a couple of saloons over in Denton. More than one of the Bass Gang trails disappeared in the area. Acting on the Pinkerton's advice the Texas & Pacific made up the train to suit the part. It consisted of the engine, wood tender, three passenger cars, a freight car, a mail car and caboose. The mail car had its usual compliment of two Pinkerton men so as not to attract any special attention. That's where ordinary ended. The passenger cars had a Pinkerton agent, Russell and two of his deputies at each end. Longstreet rode up front with the fireman where he could get the drop on anyone commandeering the engine. Cane rode in the caboose with the conductor. The freight car carried horses for Longstreet, Cane, Russell, the deputies and the Pinkertons.

They rolled out of the station on a cool spring morning under a rumpled blanket of gray cloud spitting spring showers. The first two stops proved uneventful. By the time they rolled into the third stop at Mesquite, Cane was beginning to wonder if Longstreet's planted rumor had reached Bass and his men. Mesquite was a short stop to take on and discharge passengers, mail and a small amount of freight. Cane took advantage of the stop to hit the station privy, making light of some morning coffee.

He crossed the wooden platform, bustling with the business of servicing the train. He didn't notice the lean man in a black coat with a drooping gray mustache approach the rear of the mail car as he hurried on his errand. By the time he returned, the train was ready to depart. He scrambled into the caboose while the conductor waved his signal lantern up the line to the engineer. He followed Cane into the caboose and took his seat. The customary long whistle blast announced the train's departure. Couplings engaged up the line. The caboose didn't move.

"Now what?" The conductor asked of no one in particular. He stepped out to the platform behind the car, grasped the ladder to the roof and swung around the side to have a look up the line.

"What the hell!"

Cane bolted from his seat, getting the message that something was wrong. He brushed past the startled conductor and jumped down to the platform. The mail car and the rest of the train were rolling west, gathering speed. A man in a black coat and hat climbed the ladder leading to the mail car roof. Cane drew and fired in the hope someone would hear the shot and get the idea something was wrong. The train showed no sign of slowing. No luck. The mail car rear guard had been stripped away. He spun around to the conductor.

"This is probably the start of it. Telegraph the next stop!" He looked past the depot to the sleepy little town. *Where in hell can I get a horse and fast?*

Longstreet never heard Cane's shot over the chuff of the engine and the rattle of the rails. He too was beginning to wonder if the bait for his grand trap had fallen on deaf ears.

He nudged the engineer. "How long to the next stop?"

The man with a soot-stained face popped the cover of his pocket watch.

"An hour and thirty minutes."

Longstreet settled back to wait.

★　★　★　★　★

Stillwell Russell gazed out the window of the first passenger car. The trap was taking on the feel of a fool's errand with each passing mile. A fool's errand would be bad enough without the Pinkerton man at the other end of the car there to remind him he'd end up owing the private coppers even if they failed to get Bass. He'd let Cane talk him into the arrangement over his own better judgment. Now the best case looked like a split in the reward if there ever should be one.

Arkansas Johnson crept slowly and carefully along the roof of the mail car. Dropping the caboose had been easy enough with the train at a stop. Pulling a coupler pin on a moving train would be another matter. First he had to get there without tipping off the guards below. Wind whipped a spattering of rain across the swaying car. The rain stung his cheeks and made the roof surface slippery. He dropped to his knees and crawled slowly, taking care that a boot scrape not give him away. They planned to let the train carry them out of reach of any pursuit that might have resulted from dropping the caboose in Mesquite. Sam and the boys waited another ten miles or so up the tracks. All he had to do was get in position to act on their signal.

Bass checked his watch. She should be along anytime now. The gang waited in a thicket of white oak just north of the tracks. He watched the ribbon of track to the east, waiting for the first sign of smoke against the leaden cloud bank spitting rain. There. He thought he saw something. He squinted against the rain, letting the smoke plume grow certain.

"Here she comes, boys. Mount up. Stay under cover while I give Arkansas the sign." He swung up on the blue roan and rode out of the thicket in plain sight of the tracks. A lone horseman as expected would give no alarm to the train crew or the mail car guards should they even notice.

The engineer sat in position manning the throttle. He glanced out the window. He turned to Longstreet and pointed. Longstreet moved to the platform between the engine and the wood tender. A lone horseman stood off some distance from the tracks. He saw no sign of any others. The man just sat there. It didn't look like Bass was going to take the bait. Maybe he hadn't gotten the word. Curse the luck if he hadn't. They'd gone to a lot of trouble to draw him out in the open. Kingsley had high hopes for the operation. He'd gotten Chicago involved in convincing the Texas & Pacific to go along with the charade. Railroads as a rule didn't fancy being held up, even for a good cause. Nobody was going to be happy if they came up empty-handed on this one. As the rider disappeared, Longstreet shrugged and returned to his seat.

Johnson saw the lone rider at the other end of the train. He climbed down the ladder to the mail car platform. He removed a wooden-handled hook fashioned for his purpose. He leaned over the platform rail and attempted to hook the eye opening at the top of the coupling pin. The damn thing bounced and rocked with the sway of the train rattling the rails. After a few anxious tries he connected. He stood, braced his legs and pulled. Nothing. He pulled again. The car swayed, lightly releasing tension on the coupling link. The pin came free. The mail car began to slow as the passenger cars with their posse men, Pinkerton guards and Longstreet pulled away.

Johnson sidled over to the corner of the mail car platform. He expected the guards inside might react to the car slowing down. Then again, they might just take it for the next stop and let it go at that until it was too late.

He peered around the corner of the car. Sam and the boys galloped along beside the roadbed, gaining on the mail car as it rolled to a stop. The gang drew rein beside the mail car door. A curious Pinkerton guard cracked it open to see what had caused the stop. He was greeted by four masked men with guns drawn. His eyes went wide with surprise. He cut his eyes left and right. The rest of the train was nowhere in sight. The Pinkerton men gave up without resistance. Why bother? They were outnumbered with nothing worth protecting on board.

The empty mail car threw Bass into a black rage. The robbery plan had been a stroke of genius yet all they had to show for it was wasted effort. None of the gang dared voice their anger. It was plain sure Bass had enough for all of them. They'd been tricked. Most likely the whole thing was a trap. They'd been lucky. No telling how many men were on the parts of the train they'd cut loose. He felt the long arm of the law closing in. They'd have to eat the frustration of not getting the prize they planned on. It was time to lie low for a spell.

"Handcuff and blindfold them two and let's get out of here."

They rode northeast on a wide arc, backtracking any pursuit out of Mesquite. Bass called a halt at a stream running clear with snowmelt. The gang's high expectations had turned to smoldering anger.

"That was close," Arkansas said.

Bass nodded. "I should have reckoned the leak on that shipment too good to be true."

"They fed us what we wanted to hear. They must a known we was spoilin' for a big score."

"I expect you're right. We got a might careless. It's time we lay low for a spell. Let things cool down. Word is the governor's called out a company of Rangers to go along with the Pinkertons and all the rest of them that's after us."

"Where you fixin' to hide out, Sam?" Blocky asked.

"Salt Creek. We post a lookout at Pilot Knob that gives us plenty warning of anybody comin' through the Timber Cross."

Shady Grove

"That's an amazing story. They took the train apart to rob it?"

"Brilliant really, Bass had the bollocks of a Brahma."

I scanned my notes. A golden glow told me the afternoon had advanced to quitting time. "I expect Penny will be along to fetch you off to supper presently."

"Likely so." He patted the bulge in his lap robe. "Fortunately I shall be able to muster the courage to face the tepid portions of something brown and something green they'll present us this evening."

"My pleasure to assist."

"I'm sure it is. Big plans for Sunday?"

"Hardly big, Parcheesi and sundaes if you must know."

He smiled. "Robert, do you fully appreciate everything I've done for you? You have your book coming along and a romantic interest on which to squander whatever profits might follow from it. I've fairly given you a life."

"Scarcely a day goes by."

"I'm so pleased. By the time you return next week I shall remember the Texas Rangers."

Twenty-One

Windsor Hotel
April 21
"Marshal Russell?"

"Yes." The speaker was a clean-shaven boyish-looking man of slight frame and serious demeanor. He looked the sort who might be found at home clerking in a mercantile.

"I was told I might find you here. Captain Junius W. Peak, B Company Texas Rangers. Governor Coke ordered my company to assist in the pursuit and capture of the Bass Gang."

"Welcome Captain. I've been expecting you ever since I read about the governor's order in the newspaper. Maybe your presence here will change our luck."

"Luck? I'm not sure I understand."

"Let's just say Bass and his men have been stubbornly elusive."

"Has there been any sign of them since the Mesquite robbery?"

Russell shook his head. "Nope, gone to ground without a trace as usual."

"They can't simply disappear. They need supplies. Somebody has to know where they are hiding."

"You'd think. I do have one possibility we can follow up now that you're here."

"What's that?"

"We captured one of them after the Allen holdup. He identified the other gang members. One of them is the son of a rancher in the area. I haven't had enough men to do a proper search. Now with your men here we can put that to right." He glanced over the Ranger's shoulder to the lobby door. "There's someone I want you to meet." He waved Cane over. "Captain Peak, may I present Briscoe Cane."

Peak extended his hand. Cane accepted it.

"The captain leads a company of Texas Rangers the governor has called to our assistance. Mr. Cane has been helping with the investigation on behalf of the Great Western Detective League."

"Great Western Detective League? Can't say I ever heard of it."

"Most people haven't," Cane said. "It works better that way."

"I don't understand."

Russell offered what for him passed as a smile. "Let's just say the league casts a wide net for the likes of a criminal like Sam Bass. They alerted me to be on the lookout for him a couple of months before he showed up in the area. If he'd so much as spit on the sidewalk before that first robbery, we'd have had him. That's water over the dam now." He turned to Cane. "With the Rangers here to help we can pay that visit to the Murphy ranch we're due for."

Murphy Ranch
April 29
Warm spring breezes tossed a new crop of sage as Murphy Ranch came into view. Russell called a halt on a low rise overlooking a broad grassy valley. Cattle grazed in black and brown patches scattered across the green-gold valley floor. The Murphy ranch sprawled along the southwest section a mile distant. Little could be seen beyond the hazy shadows of a low rambling ranch house, barn, bunkhouse and two nondescript

outbuildings.

"How do you plan to play this?" Peak asked.

Russell glanced over his shoulder and lifted his chin toward the ranch. "With a full company of Rangers the more interesting question is how they plan to play it. I figure we just ride on in."

Cane squinted against the sun glare. "That'll work as far as it goes. You can't hide a posse this size. They'll see you comin' sure. Give me a thirty-minute head start. I'll circle in from the south in case anyone tries to make a run for it."

"You want a squad of my men to accompany you?" Peak asked.

"That'd up the chances of me bein' spotted. I work best alone."

He wheeled Smoke west, dropped below the crest of the valley wall and rode south.

"Paw, riders comin'!"

Henderson Murphy shaded his eyes and shook his head. "Paper said the governor called out the Rangers. That's got the look of a whole company."

"Ain't no social call, Paw." Young Jim spat. "Sum-bitch Tom Spotswood ratted us out. I gotta warn Sam."

"Sam Bass can take care of his self, boy. You ride off on that errand you'll lead that posse to him sure. You need to get yourself out of here. Now saddle you a horse and git. I'll try to stall 'em."

Jim ran to the stable without looking back.

The old man stood on the front porch, a Henry rifle crooked in his arm. Russell drew a halt just beyond the yard gate.

"Have your men spread out Captain. Keep your eyes peeled

for any sign of trouble. I'll ride on in and have a talk with Murphy."

"You sure you don't want a few of us to come along, just in case."

"Best we let it rest easy for the time bein'."

"Yo the house! I'm comin' in alone." Russell eased his bay through the gate and jogged across the yard. He drew rein.

"Henderson Murphy?"

"I am."

"Stillwell Russell, US marshal. We have reason to believe your son may be involved with a recent string of train robberies. I've got a warrant here for his arrest."

"Boy ain't here."

"We've had reports that Sam Bass and his gang may be hiding in the area."

"Don't know nothin' about that."

"That so. Your son is riding with Bass and you don't know it."

"I told you. The boy ain't here. Ain't seen him in quite a spell. I figure he run off."

"Mind if we have a look around?"

"I do mind. This here's private property."

"Like I said, I have a warrant. Don't make me arrest you for obstruction."

Cane rode into a stand of white oak at the rear of the ranch house. He stepped down and ground tied Smoke. He saw no sign of movement other than a cloud of flies buzzing around fresh dropping in the corral. All eyes were likely on the company of Rangers drawn up across the front yard. He left the thicket and strolled across the yard past the house. The rear stable doors opened to a corral. Somewhere inside a horse snorted. He hugged the stable wall cat quiet as he approached the door.

A young man emerged from the shadows inside leading a horse. He started across the corral, headed for the gate at the far side.

"Hold it right there, son."

The boy froze. His hand drifted toward the butt of a .44 on his hip.

"I wouldn't try that if I were you. Now lift your hands and turn around real slow."

He turned. "Who the hell are you? You got no call to come in here givin' orders."

"You're Jim Murphy."

"What's it to you?"

"You're under arrest on suspicion of train robbery."

"That's bullshit! You ain't got no proof."

"Oh, I think we do. We got a witness."

"Spotswood." He reached for his gun. It never cleared leather. Cane's blade stuck in his forearm. His eyes went wide in shock as he stared at the bone handle.

"You stabbed me."

"Count your blessings. You could be dead." He drew his gun and disarmed the kid.

"Get this thing out of my arm."

"All in good time. Now head on out front. There's a US marshal and a company of Texas Rangers waiting to make your acquaintance."

Cane marched the Murphy boy out to the front yard.

"Look what I found, slipping out the back way."

Russell turned to the elder Murphy. "I thought you said the boy wasn't here."

Murphy returned a sullen glare.

"I'll take that rifle now. You're under arrest for harboring a fugitive."

Dallas

The posse rode into town with their prisoners under a heavy guard. People stopped what they were doing to stare. *Ain't that Henderson Murphy and his boy Jim?* Word spread through the crowd.

"Take 'em to the jail?" Peak asked.

Russell nodded.

"Hold on, Marshal," Cane said. "You gonna put him in a cell next to Spotswood?"

"I suppose."

"I got an idea. It might be best to keep those two separate until we see how it plays out."

"What are you thinking?"

"Maybe we can make a deal."

"A deal?"

"Yeah. Take 'em to the hotel. Put them in separate rooms under guard. Call a doctor to look after the kid's arm. Once he's patched up, let's have a talk with him."

Russell turned to Peak. "You get all that?"

He nodded.

"Do as he says."

The Murphy kid sat in a straight-backed chair in the corner of a room on the third floor of the Windsor Hotel. His arm was freshly bandaged. Two of Peak's Rangers flanked the door. They opened at a knock. Cane, Russell and Peak filed into the room.

"You boys can wait outside," Peak said.

The kid eyed Cane suspiciously.

"You're in a lot of trouble, Jim," Cane said. "Four counts of train robbery will put you away for a good long time. Ever been to prison?"

Murphy gave him a vacant stare.

"I'll take that for a no. Too bad, if you had you'd know just

how much trouble you're in. The boys who wind up in territo-
rial prison is a bad bunch. Pups like you don't last long in
there. Nowhere near as long as the sentence you're gonna get.
Best case you do real hard time." He drew the bone-handled
blade from the back of his holster and sat on the bed across
from the kid. He picked at a fingernail with the blade.

"They slam them steel bars on you and you're at the mercy
of your fellow inmates. Guards don't give a shit. You're just one
more mouth to feed. You best find the biggest meanest son of a
bitch you can and make yourself real nice to him. If you do, you
might last for a spell. That about right, Marshal?"

The kid cut his eyes to Russell. The marshal gave his best
somber undertaker look and nodded.

"If I was you, Jim, I'd make a deal to keep my young ass out
of that pen," Cane said.

"Deal?"

"That's right. We get what we want and we let you walk out
of here now. We don't get what we want, we lock you up with
Spotswood and you're on your way to the penitentiary and all
them nasty boys waitin' to welcome you."

"What do you want?"

"Sam Bass and the rest of the gang."

"What's that got to do with me?"

"Don't play games with me kid. You're part of the gang. You
know it and we know it. You lead us to Bass and you walk out
of here now. We get him, you walk on the charges against you.
You go back to Daddy's ranch and lead a normal life." He held
Murphy's gaze.

The kid turned to the window and gazed out at sunshine and
blue sky.

The bedsprings squeaked as Cane rose. "You let them barred
doors slam behind you and you're gonna regret this moment
for whatever little is left of your miserable life. What's it gonna

be, Jim boy?"

The kid stared out the window.

Cane shrugged. "Marshal, Captain, let's get out of here." He started for the door.

"I'll get him for you."

Cane cracked a half smile, his back to the kid. "That's more like it." He spun. The blade flashed and stuck in the window frame beside the kid's ear. Wide eyes fixed on the wavering bone handle. Cane plucked it out of the frame and returned it to its sheath. "Remember that, if you ever get a notion to cross us. Let 'em both go."

Jim and Henderson Murphy rode out of town in silence. The old man hadn't said a word when they were released. He knew something was up. They cleared town and took up a short lope for home. After a time Henderson pulled the pace down to a walk to spell the horses.

"Why'd they let us go, Jim?"

"We made a deal."

"What sort of deal?"

"I help 'em get Sam and the gang and they let me go."

"Sam Bass ain't no good, but rattin' out friends is a shameful thing. Then there's the likelihood Sam finds out and kills you."

"That's a chance I'll have to take."

"Why?"

"Cause it's a chance he kills me if he finds out. They send me to prison, Paw, ain't no chance about it."

Twenty-Two

May

A barefoot young boy in patched overalls who did odd jobs around town delivered the note to Marshal Russell's room at the Windsor. He summoned Jones and Cane to a quiet corner of the lobby bathed amber in late-afternoon light. Russell passed the note around without comment.

Salt Creek Bottoms.

JM

"Where's Salt Creek?" Cane asked.

"Denton County," Russell said. "Captain, when can your men be ready to ride?"

"First light."

"Cane?"

He nodded.

Salt Creek

They rode out the next morning at first light, Russell in the lead flanked by Cane and Jones. The Ranger column of fourteen men lined out behind. They rode east crossing grassy plain cut here and there by a network of small streams. A cornflower-blue sky and bright spring sun soared overhead. Russell set a brisk pace toward the center of the county and an area known as Timber Cross.

The column passed south under the watchful eye of the brown sandstone peak known as Pilot Knob. Bass set his watch there as others had done for decades to provide early warning of Indian attacks. Seaborn Barnes spotted the Ranger company across the plain long before it passed Pilot Knob. He had a fast horse and a good start to reach the gang's encampment in a sheltered valley along the Salt Creek Bottoms.

Barnes's horse skittered down the wooded valley wall dappled in patches of sunlight and shadow. Gang members were on their feet with guns handy when he rode into the clearing where they were camped and stepped down.

"Company's comin'. Looks like a whole company of Texas Rangers."

"Where are they?" Bass asked.

"They hadn't hit Timber Cross when I lit out. Likely have by now."

"All right boys, break camp and scatter. Work your way to the Murphy ranch. They've already checked that out. Likely won't go back before I can figure out our next move."

Russell's posse entered the wooded hill country and slowed to a deliberate pace as they neared Salt Creek Bottoms. He drew a halt below the rise leading to the valley wall.

"Hold your men here, Captain, whilst Cane and I have a look up yonder."

The Ranger company stood down. The marshal and Cane rode on. They threaded their way up the wooded slope through spears of sunlight slicing between the trees. They halted near the rim and stepped down. They ground tied their horses and crawled to the overlook.

Salt Creek cut the valley floor from north to south. Cane studied the stream banks. He spotted a blackened circle downstream from their position. He nudged Russell.

"Looks like we might be too late."

"Son of a bitch! The bastard leads a charmed life."

"Come on, let's get the Rangers and have a look around."

They collected their horses and rejoined the column.

"The camp's across the steam just south of here. It looks deserted. Captain, take some of your men and circle north, enter the valley and close down on the camp. Cane and I will take the rest and circle up from the south. If there are any of them left in the area we may get lucky."

They mounted, split the company and rode out. The south column crossed the valley wall a quarter mile south of the suspected campsite. They entered the valley and crossed the bottoms to the creek bank. As they crossed the stream and turned north Cane spotted a hoofprint in the soft bank. The fresh sign said the rider had headed southeast. He peeled away from the column and followed.

The trail climbed the wooded east valley wall under a canopy of light and shadow. Halfway up the wall it hit him. *Quiet. Too quiet.* Smoke came to a stop. He lifted his nostrils to the breeze. Cane's senses slowed as they sometimes did when he felt the presence of danger. He drew his Henry rifle from the saddle boot and rested the stock on his hip. He eased Smoke forward, his eye tracking from tree to tree, shadow and light, light and shadow. He couldn't shake the sense he was being watched.

The shot rang out as he neared the crest. A heavy-caliber bullet bit a chunk out of the white oak off his right shoulder. He leaped from the saddle and dived into cover behind the tree. A wisp of blue smoke beyond the crest to his left floated off on the breeze. He trained the Henry on that line, looking for sign of the shooter. Below and behind him further to the north he heard the faint sounds of Russell and his band of Rangers reacting to the gunshot. The shooter had to know they were there. The missed shot put him at risk. He'd run. Cane started a move toward the next tree up the slope. He felt it as much as he heard it. A horse lit out fast beyond the rim of the valley wall. He ran up the slope.

The rider bent over his horse's neck, weaving the trees to the south. He had a jump. Cane read the trail anticipating the path he might take. He guessed his spot. A hundred-yard shot if he guessed right. He shouldered the rifle, following the rider as he galloped through the trees. He'd guessed right. The rider broke into a bright sunlit clearing. The Henry barked and bucked. The rider slumped forward in the saddle. Cane lowered the rifle and whistled for Smoke with the thought he had a wounded outlaw to chase. The big gray gelding jogged up the ridgeline. The retreating rider rolled over his horse's shoulder and fell to the ground.

Cane swung into the saddle, slipped the Henry into its boot and jogged toward his fallen assailant. He drew his .44 and eased Smoke down to a walk as he approached the body. A wounded man might play possum. He saw no sign of breathing. The outlaw's gun remained in its holster. A backup was always a possibility. He cocked his .44. He drew Smoke to a stop and stepped down just as Russell and a cavalry charge of Texas Rangers cleared the ridgeline and galloped toward him. The man didn't move.

Murphy Ranch

By nightfall they began to trickle in. Bass arrived first. He rode up to the house and stepped down. Henderson Murphy stood on the porch Henry rifle in hand silhouetted in lamplight spilling from the open door.

"What the hell are you doin' here?"

"We ran into the Rangers over at Salt Creek. We need a place to hide."

"You and your men ain't welcome here no more, Bass. Jim

and I has been arrested once already on account of you. We was lucky to talk our way out of that."

"How did old Jim manage that?"

"I swore he was here at the ranch at the time of the Allen robbery. It was my word against Spotswood."

"Lucky for both of you." *And the next thing you know the Rangers show up at Salt Creek. Seems a lot to credit coincidence.*

"We need help Henderson. Your place is the perfect place for us to hide out. You've both been cleared of suspicion. The Rangers have been all over your spread. This is the last place they'll look."

"He's right, Paw." Jim stepped out of the house.

"I don't like it."

"It won't be for long," Bass said. "It's gotten too hot around here. We need to pick up some travelin' money and get shut of north Texas."

"I'll put 'em up in the bunkhouse, Paw."

The old man put up his rifle and stomped back into the house.

Jim's right about one thing. We won't be here long. Not long enough to tip off them Rangers is sure.

Jackson and Barnes rode in within the next two hours. They sat on the bunkhouse porch, watching the moon rise. Bass flipped open his watch for the third time in the last half hour.

"I don't like it. Arkansas should have been here by now."

"Maybe he's had enough and just cleared out," Barnes said.

"Wouldn't be like Arkansas. Besides we need traveling money before we blow these parts."

Jackson looked to Bass. "You don't suppose they got him do you?"

"It's possible, I'm afraid. Makes more sense than him cuttin' and runnin'."

TWENTY-THREE

Windsor Hotel

"Mr. Longstreet!"

The desk clerk waved him across the red-gold lobby glow. "We have a message for you."

He handed him a folded slip of paper.

Room 210. Come see me when you return.

Kingsley

Longstreet climbed the stairs to the second floor and made his way down the hall to room 210. He knocked.

"Come in."

The door opened to the parlor of a small suite.

"Longstreet, old boy. Good of you to come so promptly. I was just about to have a drink. Care to join me?"

"Don't mind if I do. What brings you to Dallas?"

Kingsley busied himself at a sideboard with a cut-crystal decanter and glasses. "Sam Bass, of course. We've got three railroad clients up in arms about that gang. They've got Chicago all riled up. I'm afraid we ratcheted up expectations with that gold shipment ploy. Now there's hell to pay with nothing to show for it." He handed Longstreet a glass.

"Cheers. Chicago wants results and they want them now. We need to turn up the heat. Have a seat."

Two wing chairs and a settee covered in red-and-gold brocade surrounded a low table at the center of the room. Longstreet took a seat opposite Kingsley.

"So where are we?"

Longstreet shrugged. "They disappeared like smoke in the wind after the Mesquite trap."

"Clever devils, the way they took the train apart bit by bit. Almost as if Bass knew we were onto him."

"I don't think he did. I make it out to dumb luck. Bad for us. Good for him."

"And no sign of him since?"

"None. Though not for lack of looking. The governor called out a company of Texas Rangers. The Rangers and sheriffs from three counties are all combing the hills here about looking for him."

"Any chance they've left the area?"

"It's possible, but nobody seems to think so. Cane, Russell and the Rangers pulled in a rancher name of Murphy and his son a week ago. I heard they were suspected of harboring Bass, but they ended up letting them go. They got close a couple days ago. Killed Arkansas Johnson in a shoot-out over to Salt Creek. No sign of Bass though. He's about as slippery as a mud puppy."

"Russell?"

"US marshal, Stillwell Russell. Mail robbery got him on the case. He's working with the Rangers."

"And Cane you said, he's here as well?"

"He is. We worked together on the Mesquite trap."

"What level of cooperation are we getting with this Russell chap and the Rangers?"

"We're not. To hear Russell tell it he doesn't have much use for private detectives."

Kingsley pursed his mustache, brows knit. "But didn't you imply Cane was working with them?"

"I did. Cane and Russell are thick as thieves for some reason."

"Ah. I believe I might shed some light on that. Russell may be affiliated with this Great Western Detective League Cane claims to represent. I've done a bit of investigation on that one. The whole thing is the brainchild of one Colonel David Crook. He has managed to recruit a rather extensive network of law enforcement officers to his little association. He puts the services of his operatives out for hire much as we do. They also pursue reward opportunities. They share information through the league offices in Denver and share the rewards. Quite a tidy little arrangement really. It gives local law enforcement assistance when cases go off their jurisdictions and provides bonus money based on results."

"So that's how it works."

"Perhaps we should have a chat with our friend Mr. Cane. He might be willing to cooperate for old times' sake."

"You can certainly try."

"You don't sound optimistic."

"You didn't exactly shoot straight with him the last time."

"You think he knows?"

"He knows I was already here when he arrived following the Allen robbery."

"He'd only be guessing."

"Like I said, you can try."

"Is he staying in the hotel?"

"He is."

"Let's invite him to join us for a drink in the bar."

Longstreet's invitation to meet him and Kingsley in the bar for a drink roused Cane's suspicion. He hadn't liked the Englishman from the first. His less-than-forthright exchange of information back in Buffalo Station had done nothing to improve his estimation of the man. The fact that he was here and wanting to talk was probably owing to the fact Russell had

Pinkerton frozen out of the investigation. He felt bad about that for Longstreet's sake but business is business. The Pinkertons had a reputation for grandstanding at the expense of legitimate law enforcement, most likely based on the actions of men like Kingsley. Men like Russell didn't appreciate being shown up before their superiors or in the case of others, the people who elected them. Mostly law enforcement professionals had little use for Pinkerton agents. He could talk to Kingsley, but he didn't have much to offer. He found them at a back corner table in the hotel saloon.

"Cane, good of you to join us, old boy." The Englishman rose, extended his hand and favored him with his best patent-medicine smile.

"Kingsley, what brings you to Dallas?"

"Oh heavens, you must know. Have a seat." He looked over his shoulder and waved to the bartender for another glass. He brought it over. The Pinkerton man poured.

"As you might imagine our clients and my superiors are quite anxious to see this Sam Bass affair wrapped up. Beau here has been filling me in on the most recent developments. He tells me you've managed to gain the cooperation of the law enforcement officials on the case. It seems that courtesy doesn't extend to us."

"It doesn't? I hadn't noticed."

Longstreet rolled his eyes.

"Have you then gained their cooperation?"

He nodded.

"Splendid. I was hoping we could enter into an exchange of information, for old times as it were and all that."

"Hmm, don't know that I got that much out of our last little exchange. You got something better this time?"

Guarded gates clouded the Englishman's eyes. "Yes, well nothing terribly specific at the moment. As you know I've only just arrived. I thought perhaps you might have something by way of a more recent development."

"As a matter of fact there is something."

"Excellent! I'm sure we shall be in position to reciprocate in due course."

"Oh, well I suspect that won't be necessary."

"It won't? Sorry old chap, I'm afraid I don't follow you."

"I expect we'll have the case wrapped up by then."

"I see. Well here's to success then. Cheers!"

Cane tossed off his drink. "Thanks for the drink, Kingsley." He scraped back his chair, nodded to Longstreet and left.

Longstreet watched him go. "I told you he wouldn't play along."

"Yes, well either he's bluffing or they've got on to something of interest. You said they arrested this Murphy fellow and then let him go. What was that all about?"

"I suspect it had something to do with Tom Spotswood."

"Spotswood, who's he?"

"The gang member they captured after the Allen Station robbery."

"Do you suppose this Spotswood implicated Murphy?"

"He may have."

"Then why let Murphy go? I think I should like to have a chat with this Spotswood chap."

"Slim chance of that, the sheriff's got him over at the jail."

"Oh? We shall see."

Sheriff's Office
Dallas

"Sheriff Logan? Allister Rothchild, barrister at the bar, at your service." He forced a smile.

Logan took in the distinguished gentleman in the bowler hat and tweed jacket who'd just entered his office. English he'd guess by the accent.

"What can I do for you Mr. Rothchild?"

"I understand you have my client incarcerated here."

"In car sir, what?"

"In jail, my good man, you're holding him in your jail. A Mr. Tom Spotswood."

"Your client?"

"Quite so."

"You're his lawyer."

"Why else should I be here to see him?"

"I figured the court would have to appoint someone to represent him."

"Yes well I've agreed to represent Mr. Spotswood. Now, if you please, I'd like to speak with my client."

Logan rose. "Are you armed?"

"Me? Mercy no."

"Open your coat."

He did.

"Right this way." He opened the door to a two-cell jail. "You got a visitor Spotswood."

Spotswood sat on the edge of his bunk. He scowled at the Englishman. "Who the hell are you?"

"Allister Rothchild, I've agreed to represent you."

"Agreed with who? I ain't agreed to be represented."

"I say young man you are in serious trouble here. Competent legal representation should be highly agreeable to you. Now if you please Sheriff, attorney-client privilege and all that you know."

"Spotswood?"

"I'll talk to him."

Logan closed the door and returned to his office.

"Now as I see it here you are charged with robbing the Texas Central Railroad at Allen, Texas. Is that correct?"

"What do you think?"

"I would say your incarceration speaks eloquently to that."

"What?"

"I also understand that you were caught. What is that quaint colloquialism you colonials are so fond of? Ah yes, you were caught red-handed. Now the question is what might we do to mitigate the severity of your punishment."

"What?"

"What can we do to lighten your sentence?"

"I already done that."

"Did what?"

"Told that US marshal who was in on the robbery."

"Yes, that might help. We shall have to plead accordingly. Who were your accomplices?"

"I already told the marshal."

"Mr. Spotswood, how am I to effectively represent you if you are not forthcoming with me? Now please tell me what you have previously told the marshal."

"Sam Bass is the leader. Arkansas Johnson, Blocky Jackson, Seaborn Barnes and Jim Murphy rode with us."

The Englishman knit his brow. "James Murphy of the Murphy ranch Murphys?"

"Yeah, what's it to you?"

They arrested him and then let him go. Why?

Because he is an informer!

Murphy Ranch

"Somebody's comin'." Blocky Jackson had lookout in the hayloft.

Bass looked out over the dusty road leading to town. A buggy rolled toward them behind a pair of matched blacks, trailing a dun cloud.

"Everybody get out of sight and stay out of sight until they're gone or trouble starts." The gang scattered to the barn and bunkhouse weapons handy. The buggy wheeled through the gate and up the drive to the house.

Longstreet drew the team to a halt in front of the house. He set the brake and stepped down following Kingsley up the step to the porch.

"James Murphy?" Kingsley inquired.

"Henderson Murphy, Jim's paw. Who are you?"

"Reginald Kingsley. This is my associate Beau Longstreet. Might Jim be about?"

"What do you want with him?"

"We've a business matter to discuss."

"What sort of business?" Jim appeared in the doorway behind his father.

"I should prefer to discuss it in private."

"Can't hurt to talk, Paw. Let 'em in."

The elder Murphy stepped aside allowing Kingsley and Longstreet to enter a sparsely furnished parlor. Young Murphy didn't offer them seats.

"What's on your mind?"

"We are with the Pinkerton agency."

He threw up his hands. "I been through all that with Marshal Russell and the Rangers."

"We understand that. We also understand they arrested you for the Allen train robbery and then let you go."

"That's right. Paw told 'em I was here at the ranch at the time. It was his word against Spotswood's. They didn't have no proof."

"That's not why they let you go."

Perspiration beaded up on his forehead.

"They let you go, because you made a deal with them."

The boy cut his eyes left and right. "I don't know what you're talkin' about."

"Oh, but you do, Jim. It's written all over your face. Now here's the thing, we're here to make you a better deal."

Murphy's eyes clouded. "What kind of deal?"

"A two-hundred-dollar deal."

He swallowed, his Adam's apple bobbing. "Go on."

"You tell us what you tell the marshal and we pay you two hundred dollars. We'll make it four hundred if we get there before the marshal."

"Get where?"

"Come along now Jim. We don't have time to play games. The Rangers got Arkansas Johnson at Salt Creek. We both know how they found him. That was a start. You've got more work to do." He handed him a calling card.

"I'm at the Windsor Hotel. We'll be waiting with your money."

Murphy ambled over to the bunkhouse as the buggy trailed a dusty cloud down the road back toward town.

"Coast is clear."

Bass met him at the door. "What was that all about?"

"Cattle buyers."

"Oh."

"They did have some news. The Rangers got Arkansas at Salt Creek."

"I was afraid of that. That settles it."

"Settles what?"

"It's time to get out of here. We need travelin' money. There ain't enough of us left to take down another train. We need a nice quiet, sleepy town bank. Back when I was freightin' they had a nice fat one down at Round Rock. I think maybe we should pay them a visit."

Round Rock.

Shady Grove

I arrived that Saturday morning with a sense of anticipation. I could feel the story coming to an end, I just couldn't see it. I waited impatiently in the visitor lounge. The familiar comfort of the room seemed dampened that morning by the gray light of a raw fall day. Outside a cutting wind scented with the promise of snow bestirred a rumpled flannel blanket of cloud. Winter would soon be with us. The long night would begin. I took comfort from knowing Penny would be there to help the time pass. That and the fact I should finish the book by spring.

Her heels clicked the polished floor up the long hall that led from his room past the dining hall to the lounge. She wheeled him in with a twinkle in her eye and her best Mona Lisa. I went lost for a moment.

"Good morning, Robert. I am here you know."

"Good morning, Colonel. I trust this gray morning finds you in good humor."

"I'm always in good humor. It is only the world's capacity to appreciate it that wavers."

"He can be positively incorrigible when he gets like this," Penny said.

"Dear girl, no need to put on airs for your beau at my expense. At the moment he's here to see me. You may have him when your elders are finished."

She pursed her lips and shook her head. "See what I mean? You may have him until lunchtime." She turned a hip and retreated up the hall.

"Put your tongue back in your mouth and have a seat, Robert."

He held out his hand. I passed him the bottle and tucked the empty safely away in my coat.

"I sense we are coming to the end of this story, Colonel. How do you plan to satisfy your appetites once we've finished?"

191

He smiled. "Yes I've already given that some thought, Robert."

"And?"

"All in good time. Now where were we?"

I consulted my notes. "Bass decided to rob the bank in Round Rock and get out of north Texas."

TWENTY-FOUR

Round Rock
Sunday, July 14

Round Rock sat on the Chisholm Trail at the east bank of the Brushy Creek Crossing. The settlement sprawled northeast from its roots in the heyday cattle town. A new commercial center grew up to the east leaving behind what came to be called Old Town. Bass and the gang pitched camp on the banks of Brushy Creek on the outskirts of Old Town. They sat around a small fire, taking a simple supper of hardtack, jerked beef and coffee. Stillness fell from a star-filled velvet sky. Starlight played across the rippled surface of the creek. A gentle gurgle mingled with soft night sounds punctuated now and then by the snap and pop of the fire, shooting sparks to the darkness. Finished, Bass rose and rinsed his tin plate and cup in the stream. He returned to his place by the fire.

"When do we hit the bank?" Barnes asked.

"We'll ride into town tomorrow and have a look around. We'll need to steal fresh horses. These horses are about played out. We get fresh horses we can hit the bank day after tomorrow."

Murphy smoothed his feeble attempt at a mustache. *Day after tomorrow is too soon.* "I don't like it."

"Don't like what, Jim boy?" Barnes asked.

"Stealin' horses will tip off the law to us before we get a crack at the bank. The bank's what we're after. All we got to do is rest our horses a few days. Then we jump the bank when nobody expects it."

Barnes shook his head. "Jim, Jim, Jim, why wait? No need to sit around here waitin' for somebody to stumble on us."

"Ain't no law agin' restin' horses. Steal 'em and you get people riled up."

Young Jim's advice eased some doubts. After Salt Creek and the boy's arrest Bass wondered if the kid could be trusted. He'd made sure young Jim came along on this job as much to keep an eye on him as anything. Maybe he was all right after all.

"Jim's right," Bass said. "We'll wait. End of the week should do it."

Windsor Hotel
July 15
Kingsley answered the knock at his door. It opened to a gangly young lad dressed in patched bib overalls with one shoulder strap. A slouch hat perched on a shock of unruly red hair. A splash of freckles crossed his nose and cheeks. He shifted from one bare foot to the other.

"Telegram for Mr. Kingsley." He offered a small envelope.

Kingsley took the envelope and tore it open.

Williamson County Bank, Round Rock

JM

"Have you delivered any telegrams to Marshal Russell?"
The lad shook his head.
He tossed him a quarter. "Good lad."
The boy ran off down the hall.
Kingsley crossed the hall and knocked on Longstreet's door.
"Come in."
He found Longstreet with a towel slung over one shoulder, lather on his cheeks and razor in his hand. He stroked his chin

and rinsed the razor in a basin on the dresser.

"Murphy sent word. It appears as though Bass plans to rob the Williamson County Bank at Round Rock."

Longstreet stroked the last of the lather, rinsed the razor and folded it away. He wiped his face with the towel.

"I'm on my way."

The lad in the bib front overalls found Russell having a beer with Cane in the Windsor saloon at six o'clock that evening. Russell slid the note across the table to Cane.

"I'm on my way down there first thing in the morning."

"I'll get word to Captain Peak in Austin. You can meet him in Round Rock."

Round Rock
July 17
Cane rode south on Lampasas, entering new Round Rock on the east end of town. He wheeled Smoke west on Georgetown following the central avenue through the town's commercial center. He passed the Williamson County Bank, peaceful and secure as the afternoon wore on to a three-o'clock closing. It appeared he'd arrived in time.

The first question was what to do about the bank. It seemed logical to mount a guard there. They'd have plenty of men to do that once Captain Peak and his Rangers arrived. It seemed logical then again obvious security might tip Bass off to a trap. The man either had uncanny luck or the gifts of a fortune-teller. Cane was more inclined to bet on the side of luck. He rode on past Kopperal's general store. He noted a barbershop on the corner of Georgetown and Mays. A familiar figure in a dark suit stepped out of the shop to the boardwalk. He smiled to himself. Longstreet. No grass growing under Pinkerton's feet. He drew Smoke over to the boardwalk and stepped down.

Longstreet greeted him with a grin.

"Cane, I've been expecting you. What took you so long?"

"I might ask what the hell you're doing here?"

"Same as you." He tilted his head toward the bank up the street.

"How'd you find out?"

He smiled again. "You can hold whatever opinion you like of Sir Reggie. Heaven knows I have my own reservations, but you have to give the old devil his due. He's a hell of a detective."

"You bought Jim Murphy."

"Had to find him first, besides he already had the for sale sign out. Fact is we're both here. We might just as well cooperate. Your Rangers haven't hit town yet, so for the time being, it's just you and me." He lifted his chin across the street. "Why don't you put your horse up at Highsmith's? We can have a beer on it."

Cane followed the gesture to Highsmith's Livery in the next block west.

"A beer sounds good."

"Meet me at the Saint Charles Hotel. You'll want to take a room there."

July 18

Captain June Peak reached Round Rock the next day with a detachment of a dozen Rangers. You couldn't help but notice in a town the size of Round Rock. Cane hurried down a hot dusty Georgetown to meet them. He'd spotted them the moment they hit town. He'd been at his post in Kopperal's mercantile where he and Longstreet had decided to keep watch on the bank.

"Captain Peak, glad you're here."

"Cane, we came as soon as we could. What's the situation?"

"All's quiet for the moment."

"Good. Then we got here in time."

"The first order of business is to get you and your men out of sight. You make a pretty big statement in a town this size. We don't want to tip Bass off that we're waitin' for him."

"I'll see to it."

"Good. Longstreet and I have taken up a watch on the bank from Kopperal's store across the street."

"Longstreet?"

"Yeah, the Pinkertons are here."

"How'd they get on to this?"

"Long story and I don't know the whole of it."

"I'll scatter my men around town."

"I suggest you station three or four of 'em over at Highsmith's with horses saddled and ready to ride."

"Good thought."

"Just make sure they stay out of sight."

"Do you have men inside the bank?"

"No. I decided against it. If Bass is smart he'll scout the bank first. He'd spot a heavy guard sure as hell."

"Any chance they'll try to hit it at night?"

"It's a possibility, though I don't make it likely. It'd take a hell of a dynamite charge to blow the safe. I'd use nitroglycerin if it was up to me, but who knows what would be left. You might set a night watch, but I wouldn't commit a lot of men to it."

"I'll set a watch just in case."

"You can find rooms at the Saint Charles Hotel. No tellin' how long we'll have to wait."

Shady Grove

I trudged up the street to the home buffeted by a cold wind come down from the mountains overnight. A thick blanket of gray rumpled cloud laden with the promise of snow rode east on the wind. It seemed early for such a strong prelude to winter though the calendar did say November and where the mountains were concerned, spring and fall made a thin buffer between winter cold and summer heat.

Penny. The thought warmed me. I suppose if I thought about it honestly I did owe the old scoundrel for fashioning our acquaintanceship. He'd done it of course out of his own perverse pleasure at teasing, but he'd done it nonetheless. Left to my own devices I might still be admiring the sway of her hips from afar. So be it. I owed Colonel Crook. I patted the bottle in my overcoat and climbed the wooden steps to the front entrance.

Inside the now-familiar scent of wood polish mingled with disinfectant greeted me. Rosy, who staffed the reception desk on weekends, smiled and nodded toward the solarium.

"I'll tell her you're here."

Her. A twinkle in the woman's eye suggested some unspoken familiarity with our little secret. We'd been careful. Could that be some of the colonel's mischief? He'd not be above it. The accusation evaporated moments later when Penny wheeled him down the hall. I winked at her.

"Good afternoon, Colonel. You're looking remarkably fit this fine afternoon."

"Rubbish. You know perfectly well I look like a tired old man. None of your smart-aleck sass will change a moment of that."

"Now, now, I'm sure we can find something to improve your humor." I reached for my pocket. His eyes shot wide with the horror I might expose our little arrangement. I chuckled to myself and drew out my notepad. At least I'd gotten one past him finally.

"And pray tell how that is to improve my humor?"

"Telling your stories takes you back to those glorious days and the exploits of the Great Western Detective League." I eased into a chair.

"Yes, I suppose it does."

Penny returned my wink. "I shall leave you to that then."
I watched her go.

"Oh please! Now where were we?"

I consulted my notes. "All the principals had assembled in Round Rock."

He gazed out the window at the first whispers of snow. "Ah yes. It was July nineteenth."

TWENTY-FIVE

Friday, July 19

Bass and the boys jogged into Old Town under a blazing mid-day sun. They'd decided to scout the bank one last time before robbing it during Saturday's business. As they approached the Saint Charles Hotel, Murphy called out. Bass drew a halt.

"What is it Jim?"

"My gut, Sam. You boys go along. I need to find a privy. I'll see you back at camp."

Bass nodded and led on. Murphy watched them go. He turned into the hotel rail and stepped down. He watched the gang clear the end of the street. He climbed the boardwalk and entered the lobby. He approached the desk clerk.

"I'm looking for Briscoe Cane."

"I believe Mr. Cane has stepped out."

"Mind if I wait?"

"Suit yourself."

New Town

Bass rode east on Georgetown. They crossed Mays and continued past the bank to Lampasas. They turned north, wheeled into an alley and tied up. Back on Georgetown they mounted the boardwalk and strolled west past the bank. A customer stood at one of the teller cages. No one appeared to work in the other two. A banker in a dark suit sat at a desk at the back of the lobby beside the vault. Bass noted no sign of a security guard. They crossed Georgetown and headed for Kopperal's store.

Williamson County Deputy Sheriff A.W. Grimes watched them from the southeast corner at Lampasas, his suspicion aroused. Something was up. A detachment of Texas Rangers had arrived in town the day before. They'd scattered around town clearly on the lookout for something. Then there was the Pinkerton and the Great Western Detective League operative. All these men justified carrying firearms in the face of a city ordinance forbidding it. Now these three strangers had ridden into town. Were they still more law officers or were these men in fact the reason Round Rock had turned into an armed camp? The men didn't appear to be armed. Appearances could be deceiving. *Easy enough to find out.* He started up the street.

Longstreet kept an eye on the street from the window of Kopperal's store. He'd been spared the tedium of watching and waiting by the presence of Kopperal's lovely daughter Sarah who clerked in the store. She seemed not to mind the presence of the handsome Southern gentleman who'd spent the past few days keeping watch on the bank. The three riders passing down the street brought his attention to the window. He watched the three men walk back up the street past the bank. He retreated away from the window as they crossed the street. He made eye contact with Sarah and pressed a quieting finger to his lips as the men climbed the boardwalk at the front window.

She nodded uneasy understanding. Waiting had been a pleasant diversion from the tedium of her chores. Waiting for this suddenly struck her as worrisome. He disappeared into the shelves at the back of the store. The visitor bell clanged. She gave an involuntary start, which she glossed over with a smile.

"May I help you?"

They stopped at the tobacco case, inspecting the twists and

cigars. She waited to serve them. The visitor bell clanged again. Sarah glanced at the door. Deputy Sheriff Grimes approached the taller man.

"Are you carrying a gun?"

Bass turned to appraise the deputy. He opened his coat. "Yes."

"I'll have to ask you to hand it over, your friends too if they're carrying. We have an ordinance against carrying firearms in Round Rock."

"You do? Then you'd best mosey on over to the livery stable and disarm the men over there."

"Those men are Texas Rangers. They're authorized to carry their guns."

Bass shot a recognition look at Blocky.

Barnes got it too. He drew and fired point-blank.

Sarah screamed.

Grimes's eyes went white. He clutched his gut, staggered back and slumped to his knees.

Longstreet stepped out from behind the shelves. "Sarah! Get down!"

She dropped behind the counter.

Bass and Jackson spun toward the intruder.

The Pinkerton fired.

Bass yelped, hit in the hand.

Jackson fired.

Longstreet ducked into the shadows behind the bullet gouge in the nearest shelf.

Bass held his injured wrist. "Come on! Get the hell out of here!" He led the way out the door.

Longstreet stepped out from behind the shelves, gun in hand. "Are you all right?"

The girl peeked over the counter wide-eyed and nodded.

He dashed out the door.

Mercifully the barber had completed his stroke and lifted the razor to towel the lather when the first shot rang out. Cane bolted from the barber chair. He reached the boardwalk gun in hand. Three men ran east on Georgetown toward Lampasas. Longstreet bounded out of Kopperal's store. He fired. The third man turned and returned fire. The Pinkerton dove back inside the store.

Boots clumped the boardwalk on Cane's left. He turned and leveled his gun. June Peak burst out of the International & Northern Telegraph Office gun drawn. He met Cane's eye. Cane pointed at the men fleeing up the street. Both men fired and gave chase.

Longstreet joined the pursuit up the boardwalk on the south side of the street.

The third gunman turned to return fire on Peak and Cane.

Longstreet skidded to a stop. He aimed and fired. His deliberate shot struck Seaborn Barnes in the head. He toppled to the dirt street like a fallen tree.

The remaining gunmen disappeared around the corner north on Lampasas.

Cane, Peak and Longstreet raced after them. As they reached the corner two horsemen burst from an alley up the block. They wheeled their horses north out of town. Recognition dawned on Cane. *A blue roan!* He aimed and fired.

Bass jerked in the saddle and slumped over his horse's shoulder. Slipping from the saddle he rolled into the street.

Jackson set his stirrups and drew his horse to a sliding stop. He spun the bay and fired at their pursuers.

All three men ducked back around the corner onto Georgetown. He collected Bass's horse as the outlaw leader struggled to his feet.

Somebody poked his head around the corner down the block and fired.

Jackson turned his gun on the shooter and cracked two shots. The shooter ducked back under cover.

Blocky shifted his gun to his left hand and reached down from the saddle. He grabbed Bass by the belt and hauled him up to his saddle.

"Hold your seat, Sam!"

He gritted his teeth and nodded.

Jackson spurred his horse up the street trailing dust balls behind Bass and his roan. At the end of the block he turned west, leaving his pursuers standing at the corner a block south. They galloped toward Old Town.

Cane and Longstreet exchanged glances. They turned and ran down Georgetown to Highsmith's Livery. Peak holstered his gun.

Old Town

Jackson set the pace, hoping to make it back to their camp along Brushy Creek. Bass fought the pain of his wounds, struggling to stay in the saddle. As they approached Round Rock cemetery northeast of Old Town they passed a farmhouse. Bass groaned in pain. Sensing the severity of his wounds, Jackson turned up a wooded lane. He brought the horses down to a walk and began reloading his gun. They rode on a short distance until Bass slumped forward on his horse's neck, the back of his shirt soaked in dark stain.

"I cain't go on no more, Blocky." He coughed. "I'm hit real bad."

"You can make it, Sam. Just hang on good and tight."

"No." His grip on the saddle horn slipped.

Jackson jumped from his horse to support his wounded

partner. Bass slid into his arms. Blocky's hand felt warm and sticky wet.

"Here Sam, rest a bit." He helped him off the road and propped him against a tree.

"Rest ain't gonna do it Blocky. I figure I'm done for." He coughed. His breath, ragged gasps. He spit blood. "You need to take my horse and get out a here."

"Your horse?"

"He's the best we got."

"I ain't leavin' you, Sam."

"Listen to me." A coughing fit choked him with pain. "You gotta. There ain't no other way. Now go."

"But . . ."

"But nothin'. Git!"

The order brooked no disagreement. He collected the blue roan, stripped off Bass's tack and laid it near his fallen leader. He unsaddled his horse and settled his tack on the roan. He swung into the saddle. His eyes welled. Bass rested against the tree, his eyes half-lidded against the pain, his skin chalky pale.

"You take it easy, Sam."

His eyes fluttered. "Sure, sure, ain't too dark yet. Now go on, go."

He wheeled the roan and loped up the shaded lane.

Round Rock

Jim Murphy heard the shooting. He left the Saint Charles lobby, collected his horse and rode into New Town to investigate. A body lay in the street surrounded by a gathering crowd. He saw no sign of Bass or any of the boys. He rode up to the crowd. He recognized the dead man. Captain Peak stood by with three of his Rangers. Murphy stepped down and approached him.

"What happened?"

Peak lifted his chin to the corpse. "This one and two others shot Deputy Sheriff Grimes over at Kopperal's store. They made a run for it. Some of us gave chase. The Pinkerton shot him. You know him?"

"Seaborn Barnes. What happened to the other two?"

"They got away. One of 'em took a bullet. It looked like he got shot pretty good. You know who they might have been?"

He nodded. "Sam Bass and Blocky Jackson. You goin' after 'em Captain?"

"Not enough light left. We'll head out in the morning."

Old Town

Cane and Longstreet rode west toward Old Town. They came up on a run-down farmhouse. An older woman stood in the yard hanging laundry out to dry. Longstreet drew rein and tipped his hat. He flashed his most disarming Southern smile.

"Afternoon, ma'am. Beau Longstreet. This here is Briscoe Cane. We're on the trail of a couple of outlaws that shot Deputy Grimes back in New Town. We believe they've come this way. Might you have seen anything?"

"You the law?"

"I'm with the Pinkerton agency, ma'am. Mr. Cane here is a bounty hunter."

"Who you after?"

"We believe one of them to be the notorious train robber, Sam Bass. He's now wanted for murder in addition to his other crimes."

She knit her brow, weighing civic duty and well enough alone. "I seen a couple of men pass this way."

"How long ago?"

"Not long."

"Which way did they go?"

"Headed up yonder toward the cemetery. One of 'em looked like he might need it soon enough."

"Much obliged, ma'am." He tipped his hat. They rode on.

As they prepared to skirt the cemetery east of Old Town, Cane noticed fresh horse sign leading up a tree-lined lane to the north. He drew a halt and stepped down for a closer look. He found fresh blood mixed among the hoofprints.

"They went this way."

He remounted and led the way north. A half mile up the tree-lined lane, they made out a man propped against a tree. He appeared to be sleeping or dead. Cane drew his gun. Longstreet followed his lead. They rode on. As they drew near, Cane signaled a halt.

"Keep him covered." He stepped down to approach on foot.

The man's chest rose and fell, his breathing ragged. His eyes fluttered open. He squinted to focus his gaze. Death's pallor haunted his skin. Recognition registered dull light.

"I'm Sam Bass."

"Are you armed?"

"Armed? I'm near killt."

"What happened to the man who was with you?"

"I sent him on his way."

Cane spoke over his shoulder. "Best go find us a wagon, Beau."

"You sure?"

"Yeah. Dyin' men don't lie much."

Longstreet toed a stirrup and squeezed up a lope back to New Town.

Cane knelt beside the outlaw. "You led us on one hell of a chase, Sam."

"Freighted some around these parts." He coughed. Blood trickled down his chin at the corner of his mouth.

"That's just this last turn. I been after you since Deadwood."

Bass managed something between a crooked smile and a

grimace. "Then you've had one hell of a chase. What's your name?"

"Briscoe Cane."

"You the law Briscoe Cane?"

"Bounty hunter."

"What does a bounty hunter want with the likes of me?"

"You bought yourself quite the reputation, Sam. Folks with deep pockets want to see you brought to justice."

He closed his eyes. "It's a comfort to feel wanted when you're killt. Who are these rich friends of mine?"

"Wells Fargo, Union Pacific, Texas Central, just to name a few."

He choked. "How much they think I'm worth?"

"All totaled, three maybe four thousand."

"I guess that sounds pretty good in your line of work."

"Worth my time and trouble."

"That's the difference between us, Cane. While you was chasin' me for three or four thousand, I took eighty thousand off just them first two friends you mentioned."

"And got yourself killt for it."

Bass clenched his eyes against a wracking cough. "I reckon there is that."

"Might be best if you made peace with your Maker instead of jawin' with me."

Bass lifted a brow. "You a bounty hunter or a preacher?"

"No law says a bounty hunter can't be God-fearin'."

"I suppose not. A God-fearin' bounty hunter is one thing, a God-fearin' train robber is another."

"You still got time."

"I don't expect your God would have much call for the likes of me."

"Oh I don't know, He made a place for one good thief. I expect He might have room for one more. Never hurts to ask for pardon. You'd ask the governor if you was sentenced to hang."

"I'll think on it some."

Blocky Jackson watched the scene play out from the shadows of the trees up the lane. An hour later the big Pinkerton returned with a wagon, a Ranger escort and a familiar figure riding with them. *Jim Murphy, what's he doin' with them? It don't appear he's under arrest. What the hell's goin' on?* Then it hit him. *Judas Jim Murphy.*

He watched as they loaded Bass into the wagon. Even from a distance he could see death's gray pallor stalk his friend.

Judas Jim Murphy sold us out, Sam. I'll get him. If it's the last thing I do, I'll get the son of a bitch.

Round Rock

July 21

Longstreet paused at The Crossing Saloon bat wings. He swept a quick look around the dimly lit smoky haze. Cane sat at a back corner table. He pushed through and strode across the scarred plank floor, the sound of his boot heels lost below the low hum of gambling, grumbling and girls giggling for hire. Cane glanced up as he pulled back a chair.

"He's gone."

He nodded and poured the Pinkerton a drink. "Tough hombre. Lasted longer than a man shot that bad should by rights."

"No need to wait around for a trial before collecting those rewards."

"Nope, no need."

"How much you figure it adds up to?"

He shrugged. "Bass got so notorious I kinda lost count. Between Wells Fargo, Union Pacific, and them two Texas railroads I expect the colonel will have us a pretty fair payday by the time I get back to Denver. Course we didn't recover all the UP gold, but we got us a fair share of it. I figure my part might come to three thousand or so. How about you?"

"Me?"

"Yeah, you got Barnes. That should be good for somethin'."

"Pinkerton will pocket whatever that amounts to. All I got was a congratulatory telegram from Kingsley."

Cane lifted his glass. "Don't spend all that in one place." He knocked back his drink and poured another round.

"I tell you Beau, you're wastin' your time workin' for that outfit. The Eye that Never Sleeps, that's you all right. Old man Pinkerton pockets the rewards for your work and gets a good night's sleep to boot."

"It's a living."

"Hell, why not come back to Denver with me? Talk to the colonel. I'll put in a good word for you. We make better partners than competitors."

"Denver, hmm. I might just do that after a spell."

"What spell?"

"After I spend some time in Buffalo Station."

Cane threw him a knowing twinkle in his eye. "Come on, boy, I'll buy you some supper."

"You can afford it."

"I can."

Denver

1908

Morrison's Café wasn't fancy. The food was good and the service included table linen. By the time Friday night rolled around I'd had about all the waiting a man in love could stand for a week. I'd taken to escorting Penny to dinner, where we planned our weekend outings. I found my weeks revolving around our time together. That included the charade we played for the benefit of her colleagues at the Shady Grove Rest Home and Convalescent Center. Colonel Crook of course knew the truth of our courtship, but his silence could be bought for a blessing by a weekly bottle of contraband whiskey, so long as my lovely attendant didn't find out.

We were seated at a candlelit corner table one frigid February Friday night I well remember. She looked lovelier than usual, though I must confess that may have had something to do with my appetite for loveliness that evening. We'd toasted the evening with a second glass of sherry while awaiting the serving of a German chocolate cake that had become an unlikely favorite for my Irish girl. When I'd made so bold as to observe that, she informed me that chocolate *transcended nationality*. I stood corrected.

"Will you be along to see him tomorrow?"

"Of course."

"And how is the book progressing?"

"We've finished the Sam Bass story."

"Oh. What then?"

"The colonel created quite a remarkable agency with his Great Western Detective League. We've only written the first case. His ramblings and my rummaging in the newspaper archives tell me he recruited a fascinating network of operatives with more tales to tell."

"You think then you have more than one book here?"

"I hadn't put it quite like that before. Yes, quite likely I think. I've more work to do to complete this story of course. Then there is the small matter of finding a publisher."

"Oh Robert, I've no doubt you shall. You shall have a wonderful career as an author."

She saw the future as I hoped to see it. Suddenly it occurred to me I might see it with her. I may have choked on a bite of cake at the thought. It had a rather permanent ring to it.

When I walked her home after supper, I saw her turned-up nose profiled in the streetlamp differently somehow. When we climbed the step to her rooming house, I kissed her sweetly as was my custom. Ardor came upon us in a rush. I feared it frightened her as much as it surprised me. I held her close. She held me just as close, not too terrified by the moment. We stood there warm in the cold. Fresh snowflakes began to fall. I brushed a few from her cheeks, kissed her more chastely and left. I considered a world of new possibilities on the long cold walk to my own solitary room that night. It did indeed appear a world of new possibilities was opening to me; and for Colonel Crook, an assured supply of his weekly whiskey ration.

"All in good time, my boy, all in good time."

AUTHOR'S NOTE

Sam Bass and Joel Collins terrorized the Cheyenne & Deadwood stage in 1877. On September 18, along with Bill Heffridge, Tom Nixon and others, they robbed a Union Pacific train at Big Springs, Nebraska. The gang made off with sixty thousand dollars in newly minted twenty-dollar gold pieces. Collins and Heffridge were killed in a shoot-out with a posse a week later at Buffalo Station in Kansas. Bass escaped to Texas where he soon resumed his outlaw career. A string of train robberies attracted the attention of law enforcement including US Marshal Stillwell Russell, a company of Texas Rangers and Pinkerton agents. Sam Bass was fatally wounded in a shoot-out in Round Rock, Texas, on July 19, 1878, after being betrayed by gang member Jim Murphy. He died two days later.

While certain characters and events of these stories have a basis in historical fact, the author has taken creative license in characterizing them. The Great Western Detective League is loosely based on General David J. Cook's Rocky Mountain Detective Association. The names have been changed to allow the author, along with those who record history, to spin a yarn for the entertainment of the reader. Where there is any conflict between historical assertion and the author's interpretation, it is the author's intent to present a fictional account for the enjoyment of the reader.

ABOUT THE AUTHOR

Paul Colt favors Unexpected History, stories that have some little known or overlooked aspect to otherwise familiar characters or events. His analytical insight, investigative research and genuine horse sense bring history to life. His characters walk off the pages of history into the reader's imagination. His style blends Jeff Shaara's historical dramatizations with Robert B. Parker's gritty dialogue.

Paul's first book with Five Star, *Boots and Saddles: A Call to Glory,* received the Marilyn Brown Novel Award, presented by Utah Valley University for excellence in unpublished work prior to its release in 2013. His *Grasshoppers in Summer* received Finalist recognition in the Western Writers of America 2009 Spur Awards.

Paul's work in Western fiction gives creative expression to a lifelong love of the West. He gets his boots dirty researching a story, whenever possible from the back of a horse.

Learn more at www.paulcolt.com.